the Virgin

REVENGE

REDEMPTION

Shiloh Walker

REVENGE

I was seventeen when I met Drake Gallagher. Seventeen, naive, foolish...and in love. Or so I thought. That summer, and the months that followed, set the course of my life.

Ten years later, I'm still struggling to put the pieces of me back to together. It's time to stop struggling. It's time to take control...and maybe, it's time for a little revenge.

He doesn't have time for naive little virgins? Well, I'm not naive anymore.

———————◉———————

REDEMPTION

THEY SAY REVENGE IS a dish best served cold. Maybe that's why my plans didn't work out. Cold could never describe what I feel for Drake Gallagher. Still, after ten years of bitterness, ten years of hiding in the shadows, I'm not sure there's any way to bridge the distance between us. Especially now.

Running away seemed to be the best answer. So what am I supposed to do now that he's found me again? Is it time to open up and tell him...everything? The safest thing to do would be push him away. But safety is an illusion. Nobody knows that better than me.

"You don't need to see me in."

He cocked a brow. "Perhaps there is something I need to discuss with you."

Barely, I managed to keep from curling my lip at him. Just barely. I slid inside and disarmed the alarm as he shut the door behind me. My heart hammered in my chest, that silly, foolish little fantasy settling in my mind again. Him kneeling before me, his mouth on mine.

Another kiss.

His body pressed to mine.

Him fulfilling that promise he'd made all those years ago.

Hurtful words undone. Could that happen? Could we go back to who we had been on the beach, him a too-solemn, serious young man and me a foolish, hopeful girl who hadn't had her heart, her dreams, her world smashed, all within the span of a couple of months?

Was this why I was here?

Was *that* why I had come here, seeking him?

What would closure give me, I wondered. The loss will be there. The pain will not fade. And everything he took from you will still be his.

No. I didn't need closure. I needed to end this, because this would solve nothing.

Taking a deep, bracing breath, I turned.

And the breath stuttered out of me as I found him just scant inches away, his face lost in the shadows. "Mr. Gallagher," I said, his name catching on my lips.

"Drake." He reached up, flicked a lock of hair behind my ear.

My heart skittered inside my chest and the ache within me spread.

"Drake. I—"

"You didn't ask what the inappropriate things are," he murmured, moving even closer, until even the *thought* of personal space died. I could feel the heat of him, so close, warming my skin. Under the silk of my dress and the strapless bra I wore, my breasts ached, feeling too full, while my nipples went tight. And my thighs felt like putty. Leaning back against the table, I braced my weight on my hands and tried to pierce the darkness to better see his face.

"I beg your pardon?"

"You never asked," he said, his heat crowding in around me, his scent flooding my head and it was like I was lost. Again. Lost in the time, years ago, when life was simple and easy and sweet. When things made sense and there was no pain. Just me, just him, and the promise of the life I'd thought would be mine.

He reached up and cupped my cheek, so close that all I could see was the gleam of his eyes. "Is this inappropriate?" he murmured, his mouth just a whisper away, our breaths mingling.

A warning alarm sounded in my head.

Dedication

To those I love. I thank God for you.

Copyright

2013 © Shiloh Walker
Originally published under the pseudonym
J. Dallas
as
The Virgin:
REVENGE & REDEMPTION

———◦◉◦———

Editorial Work by Deelylah Mullin

———◦◉◦———

Part One

Revenge

Chapter One

A LOT OF SKYSCRAPERS jutted up into the sky like the typical erect phallus, a sort of monument to the male species. Not Gallagher Enterprises. It flowed. There were sleek lines and soft colors. It was ivory and all those windows were like a thousand jewels under the sun. Something about it made me think of a woman. Not that it was feminine.

Perhaps it was that Drake Gallagher— the man who'd designed the building— decided he'd rather spend his time inside a building that appeared to be a tribute to feminine strength, not just another phallic symbol. Who knew.

Or maybe he wanted his company's headquarters to stand out.

The Boy Genius had always had a head for things like that.

He'd been called that for a long time—I'd heard the whispers even when he'd first appeared in my small corner of the world and it had secretly thrilled me. After, I'd wished I'd been a little less the naïve fool he'd accused me of being and paid more attention to all those little whispers. Maybe it would have given me some sort of clue.

Drake Gallagher was no longer any sort of *boy*.

He was thirty-four now. Back then, his hair had been longer, a deep shade of red that women would spend serious sums of money on, just trying to achieve that color. His was natural and the sun would tease out a dozen other shades, even as it warmed his skin to a smooth, golden glow. He'd been leaner then, long, almost lanky, but in the past ten years, that long, lean body had changed in the most delicious way. He was still long and lean, but his shoulders were wider and there was a hint of a powerful body underneath those beautiful suits he wore. I hadn't seen him except in a few interviews on TV, and more than dozen pictures in various trade magazines, but I could see the changes.

If life were fair, he would have grown softer, not harder.

But life was often not fair.

He was more beautiful now than ever.

Probably still as cruel, though. I needed to be on my guard.

I pulled out my compact, checked my make-up, my hair one last time as I climbed from the cab. I'd had nightmares the night before, but I had a deft hand with cosmetics and one wouldn't see the sleepless night just by looking at me. I knew how to hide those rough nights—a skill I'd been forced to pick up. Nightmares had plagued me off and on for the past ten years, although they happened less often now. Stress brought them on. Today, I certainly had reasons to be stressed.

In twenty-eight minutes, I had an interview. His administrative assistant was leaving the company—she had recently married and was pregnant. It was pure luck I'd managed to secure an interview. Luck, or perhaps fate giving me a chance to get back some of the pride he'd ripped out of me all of those years ago.

Before I put the mirror away, I stared into my eyes. They were the one thing that hadn't changed over the years. Would they give me away? Ten years ago, they had been innocent, naïve. *Innocent* might still apply in some ways, but naivety had died that day on the beach.

In the months that would follow, even *hope* would die.

No, I decided after a careful study. Not even the eyes were the same. The color, the shape. But there were a thousand, a hundred thousand brunettes out there with gray eyes. Maybe they didn't all have eyes shaped like mine, tilted up a bit at the corner, and maybe those brunettes didn't have the same smattering of freckles across their noses. Everything else was different, though. At seventeen, I hadn't wanted to waste time on things like make-up or hair. It was unusual for my hair to grow an inch or two past my chin at that age and if my mother wasn't quick enough to offer a cut, then I'd hack away at it myself. There had been a softness to my face, a light in my eyes.

All of that was gone now, lost to time as the soft happy girl I'd been slowly faded and died.

I knew what people saw as I strode through the doors, my heels clicking on the floor. The girl I had been spent her summers helping with the hotel, cleaning the rooms to prepare for new arrivals, or even assisting with repairs. Come afternoon, I'd be on the beaches. My hair had grown sun-streaked from so much time on the beach, and my wardrobe consisted of shorts and tank tops. I'd carried probably an extra twenty pounds then, but it hadn't bothered me. It wouldn't bother me now, either. The problem was that very little interested me—not food, not life, nothing.

Except this.

This had been the end goal for so many years.

The softness of my youth had melted away; lack of interest in life had stripped away those extra twenty pounds, plus a few more. I was now more slender than I needed to be, but it wasn't a disadvantage in this life. Over the years, I'd learned, painstakingly, how to dress to flatter my new figure.

As a teenager, my breasts and hips had annoyed me—I had been the ultimate tomboy, right up until I foolishly fell in love.

I'd left the foolishness, and that girl, behind.

———————◈———————

AS I STOPPED IN FRONT of reception, I didn't fidget. That was a habit, one of many, I'd forced myself to break. I didn't let myself check the hem of the gray silk suit and I didn't look at the time as I waited for the pretty blonde. When she looked at me, I smiled. "Hello. I have an appointment at 8:30."

"You're here for Mr. Gallagher, then." She nodded, handed me a guest pass and signaled to a man in a conservative black suit.

A few minutes later, I found myself in a room with half a dozen other women. It was to be a group interview. If I hadn't already heard how he did things, it would have thrown me off. I might not have let that show, but I was glad I'd done my research. I'd been watching, watching and waiting for this chance for years.

As I settled in one of the available chairs, I studied the women.

They weren't exactly my competition. Either I would get the job, or I wouldn't.

One of the main reasons I'd applied for this position was simply for the chance to see him, to face him. After all of this time.

Should he even offer me the position, he'd do a background check and he'd learn who I was. Assuming he hadn't already done that. Perhaps he'd forgotten. Perhaps I hadn't mattered enough for him to remember.

He'd ruined my life, and in the months that followed, I'd lost everything that mattered. I had every reason to remember him.

He had no reason to remember me.

It was a thought that settled in the back of my mind and refused to leave over the next twenty minutes as we waited.

Another woman, a beautiful blonde with a suit that was just a little too tight, settled in the seat next to mine as I brooded. She crossed her legs, reached up, freed one button. I eyed it, debated.

She sighed and studied the ceiling. "A group interview," she muttered. "I wasn't ready for that."

"It's not unheard of. Saves time, puts us on edge. And I've heard that he's...eccentric," I offered.

She snorted, then looked around, staring at the others. I could see the nerves blooming in her eyes. The other women were more polished than she was. One of her nails looked like she'd been chewing on it. Absently, I reached into my bag and pulled out a file, shaped up two nails that didn't need it, then offered it to her.

She stared at it. Then, with a sigh, took it. I went back to studying the group.

"I need this job," she said abruptly.

I blinked, then looked back at her.

She grimaced. "I guess that's not anything we should say to each other."

I shrugged. "We all need the job." I paused, then held out my hand. "I'm Shannon. Shannon Crosby."

"Beth Gibbens." She tugged at the hem of her suit. "I don't fit in."

"Don't fidget." I glanced over, past a blonde who was a more polished version of Beth. Her suit fit better and if I had to make a bet on it, I'd say her haircut had cost about two hundred bucks. She looked like smooth and elegant sex. Our gazes locked and she crossed her legs, a smile curving her lips before she shifted her gaze to Beth. The smile took on a derisive slant before she shifted her attention elsewhere.

The derision annoyed me.

Looking back to Beth, I said softly, "The key is not to fidget. If you do that, you look like you lack confidence and that is more of a turnoff to employers than anything else."

Beth laughed nervously. "How about desperation?"

"That, too."

There was no time for anything else. The man who'd escorted me into the room opened the door and we all rose.

As we headed to the door, the blonde with the pricy cut somehow managed to drive the spike heel of her shoe into my toe. I locked my jaw to keep from saying anything.

Then, as we filed down the hall, I caught Beth's elbow.

"Button it." I nodded to her blouse.

She stared at me.

"Trust me."

With my foot throbbing, I filed down the hall after the rest.

THE RIDE TO THE EXECUTIVE levels was quiet, but far from easy. The tension was palpable, thick enough to cut with a knife. My head was pounding from the lack of sleep, too much perfume, the scent of hair products clouding the air. Sweat broke out along my spine, sliding down to pool at the base, just below the loose-fitting waistband of my skirt.

This was it.

It didn't matter if I got the job.

All I had to do was see him.

Look at him.

It would help if he looked at me and *felt* something.

I knew the look in his eyes when he was attracted. I'd seen it before. If he could look at me and feel that pull, that tug I'd felt then...if he could feel that, even if he didn't act on it, then I could feel better.

Maybe it would give me something back.

It wouldn't be enough.

Nothing would ever be enough.

But I'd learned to settle for what I could get, a long time ago.

The doors opened and I fought the urge to heave out a sigh of relief as I escaped the press of the other women. Beth remained at my side and I reached up, hooked my arm through hers. "Just think. In another hour or so, it will be over," I said, keeping my voice low.

A surprised laugh gurgled out of her. She glanced at me. "You don't exactly sound like you *want* the job."

I shrugged. "I'm here, right?"

The doors in front of us were stamped metal, an elegant design that caught the eye and refused to let go. Forcing myself to look away, I watched as the doors swung inward.

There he was.

It was, in short, a fist, straight to my heart, seeing him again.

He wasn't even facing me, but I felt the impact of his presence, even from here. Standing at the end of the table, his back to us, I noted his hair was still that deep, burnished red, shorter than it used to be, yet long enough for a woman to plunge her hands into, tangle her fingers in it as he kissed her senseless. And he could do that, I knew for a fact. Nobody else had ever been able to steal the breath from me with something as simple as a kiss.

Don't think about his kisses.

It was almost impossible not to, but I managed.

His suit, a deep, deep gray, stretched over wide shoulders, fitting him to perfection. I knew how those shoulders looked without the suit, how his skin bronzed under the sun—it wasn't fair, really. He was a redhead. If fate was fair, he should freckle. Instead, he tanned. *I* freckled, or burned.

Although I could only see the barest edge of his profile, my heart slammed hard against my ribs.

Don't do that. Stupid, stupid heart. I'd had a good, long hard talk with myself this morning. I had a goal in mind, a mission. If by some stupid twist of fate I ended up *getting* this job, I had a mission. I wanted to see him feel as I'd once felt. Miserable, empty.

How I'd accomplish that, I didn't know, but that was what I wanted.

I'd never get there if my heart got mixed up again. I couldn't let myself keep remembering how I'd once felt about Drake Gallagher.

But here I was, my heart pounding away, the same way it had when I was seventeen.

And he hadn't even looked at me.

He nodded, absently reached up to brush a thumb down his jaw as he spoke to the woman before him. She was slender, her midnight hair swept into an elegant knot. Her hand rested on the high mound of her belly, and she nodded at him before turning her dark eyes to look at us.

Her gaze bounced off me, lingered on the blonde who'd smashed my foot, moved to Beth. Measuring up each one of us.

Normally, I'd watch her, subtly, try to figure out how we were stacking up in her eyes.

But Drake had turned around.

And for the first time in ten years, I was looking into the eyes of the man who'd destroyed my life.

Chapter Two

HIS EYES WERE A PURE, almost crystalline green. When he'd been in Massachusetts, spending hours on the beach with me, his skin had deepened to that warm, golden glow and it had made his eyes practically gleam.

They still had that powerful impact now, but his gaze didn't linger on me— not even for a second— and I sat there, curling my fingers into fists under the table as he spoke to each of us individually, then addressed the group as a whole.

Vaguely, through the buzzing in my ears, I heard his words, understood them.

A group interview, as I'd expected. Lovely.

The rest of my mind was elsewhere.

I nodded and smiled and made the appropriate noises as the interview started, but in reality, my mind spun in circles as I tried to figure out what to do, how to handle this.

He hadn't recognized me. At all.

My belly was a sick, twisting little mess of despair and I thought about rising, walking away. Just walking away. I didn't need to do this, didn't need to be here. I could find another job, and even if it took a while, it wouldn't matter.

But then his eyes came back to mine, and for a moment, just a moment, his gaze lingered. Memories— of the way it had felt to have those eyes burning into me, his weight pressing against me as our hearts raced— rose inside me.

He'd once made me feel like I was *everything*.

Then he cut me down to nothing.

Now, he looked at me like I was just...anybody. That look, lingering for just a second, was all I had to hold on to. Not much of a thing. Not much of a hope.

But that connection, faint as it was, while our gazes locked, made my heart race and my palms went damp.

Had I really come this far just to walk away because he didn't *know* me?

Really?

Resolved, I straightened in the chair and forced my brain to focus.

———◉———

GROUP INTERVIEWS WERE all about competition, standing out from the crowd.

They also made the candidates nervous as hell.

It didn't really help that I was already nervous, already on edge, my skin tight and prickly under the sleek cut of my gray suit. But I could handle the nerves, could handle the pressure just fine. Group interviews weren't unknown to me and I knew why they did them. They saved time, let the employer find out who worked well under fire.

I couldn't help but feel sorry for some of the women there. It was pretty obvious several of them hadn't ever had to handle a situation like this; when they were asked, in front of the others, questions like, *Why do you think we should hire you over any other candidate in this room*...it was clear they didn't know how to handle it.

My foot throbbed as the woman who'd smashed it stood up to introduce herself. Maybe I should thank her. The minor pain was something else to focus on as I forced my tense muscles to relax.

Her name was Anna Simone. Lovely. She did a bang-up job and managed to convey her skills well, and when she looked at Drake, her eyes warmed. She leaned forward as she spoke, explaining her skills, just *why* she should get this job...and she managed to convey, without really saying it, just how *much* she'd be willing to do. Her gaze never left his.

I saw the chill settle in his eyes, watched as a subtle shift took place on his current admin's face. The admin's name was Mai Nhu and her brow rose ever so slightly before she looked down at her iPad to make a note.

Oh, honey. You just lost your chance. Anna didn't even seem to realize the atmosphere had just changed, though, and she continued on, listing her experience, her past jobs, before going on to explain why she was the best candidate for this job.

Anna paused briefly to give Drake or Mai a chance to ask questions and while he was silent, Mai gave her a polite smile. "Thank you, Ms. Simone."

The interviews droned on. I had my chance near the end. I barely remembered how I did. I can remember looking Drake in the eyes. I can remember looking Mai in the eyes. And I can remember the feel of the wind on my face, the way tears had mingled with saltwater one day ten years ago. I looked into his eyes as I finished answering yet another spate of questions. *You don't remember me at all, do you?*

There was nothing in his eyes.

Absolutely nothing.

———◈———

"WE WOULD LIKE TO SPEAK a bit longer with Ms. Crosby and Ms. Gibbens."

The interview ended with that simple statement.

Beth and I looked at each other.

Everybody else looked at us.

Then they rose, filed to the door, save for Anna.

"Can I expect a return interview?"

She directed the question to Drake.

Mai responded with a polite, "It's unlikely, Ms. Simone, but thank you for your time."

"But—"

"Please make sure to turn in the visitor badge." Mai's voice was polite, but so very firm. I could like her. A lot.

A moment later, the doors shut again. Beth and I waited.

"Ms. Gibbens, your resume is impressive, but I don't think this is the right job for you. However, I do have an opening that I think will suit you." Drake flipped through the resume.

I studied him from under my lashes. It was odd, I thought, the head of the company handling this. I could see him hiring his own admin. He had to work with that person, day in and day out.

"Sir?"

He glanced up, smiled. "My local head of HR needs a new assistant. Her administrative assistant is retiring shortly. We didn't get much notice and we don't have much time to get somebody hired, either. Normally, we'd look within to promote, but...well, I have reasons to think you would do the job best. I prefer to have the best, especially within HR. You have extensive experience within that field."

Beth nodded. "Yes, Mr. Gallagher."

He nodded, glanced at Mai. "See if Hannah has any time to speak with Ms. Gibbens." He looked back at Beth. "We'll have to set up the interview, see how it goes. I'm sorry this didn't work out but I believe in having people in the right position."

"I completely understand." She smiled.

If I wasn't mistaken, she looked a little relieved.

I couldn't blame her. Working with Drake would be a pain in the ass.

———⚬———

A FEW MINUTES LATER, I realized that pain in the ass was about to be a pain in *my* ass. Unless I decided this was enough.

He sat across from me, the brilliant rays of sun coming in through the window behind him, gilding that beautiful hair of his, casting too much of his face into shadow, while he leaned back in his chair.

Mai had left, briefly.

I had no doubt the ever-efficient woman would be back.

But for now, I was alone. *Step into my parlor...*

"You're from Massachusetts," he said, his eyes resting on my face. My resume was in front of him, but he didn't look at it.

I inclined my head.

"After you graduated, it doesn't look like you went back there."

"There was no need." *No reason.* Everything that made it home was gone.

"Not even for a visit?"

Something in his voice...what was that? I tried to catch something of what he might be thinking, feeling, but with the sun at his back it was almost impossible to even see him, much less gauge what might be in his mind. I almost wanted to believe he remembered, but if he did, why was he going on like this? Crossing my legs, I smoothed down my skirt, a momentary ploy for time before I answered. "No, Mr. Gallagher."

It was a small lie, but he didn't need to know that. I did go back. Every year. For one day only.

He nodded and then leaned forward, studying my resume again before flicking me another look.

"This position is going to require long hours. If I'm here at seven, I expect you to be here as well."

Arching a brow, I said, "That isn't an issue."

"Very often, I *am* here at seven, and I'll work past eight. That's five days a week. And it's not unusual for me to be here for five or six hours on Saturday, either. If I'm working, you're working."

"Again, not an issue." My heart slammed against my ribs. He was considering giving me the job. He hadn't recognized me.

A memory swam up from the depths of my mind. Those cool green eyes, flicking my way, my mouth still buzzing from that last, burning kiss, my skin heated, my breasts throbbing. *I don't fuck naïve little virgins, Shan.*

I'd gone by the nickname *Shan* for the longest time. I'd been named after my father and it was confusing, having two Shannons. *Shan* had suited me. Until my heart was shattered, until my world was ripped out from under me. Until the dreams on which I'd built my entire childish life dissolved in front of me, like cotton candy in the rain. Total destruction came later, but that...that had been the start of it.

Brushing the memory aside, I continued to watch him.

The door behind us opened and although I didn't hear her, I knew Mai had returned. "I'm sorry for the delay, Mr. Gallagher."

He didn't even respond, just continued to watch me.

After a moment, he said bluntly, "I lost four assistants in the fourteen months before I finally found Mai. You will have no social life. I'm being honest here. I pay well for the sacrifice, but there is a sacrifice. My work is my life and there's no getting around it. Since I need a full time admin, you'll have about as little time for a life as I do. If that's a problem, you should let me know now. It's possible we'll have another position for you in the company."

"I applied for this one." I glanced past him, my gaze lingering on Mai for a moment. She'd managed to find time to get married, even if he did work people into the ground. I thought about pointing that out, but didn't bother.

He rose from behind the desk, came around to study me. "You won't be disappointing a boyfriend, a husband?"

That wasn't very subtle of him. Letting a faint smile curve my lips, I said, "Perhaps it would be a girlfriend I was disappointing."

That caught him offguard.

Mai chuckled. "Well, regardless of your significant other, they won't see a lot of you. You need to keep that in mind. The hours are the reason I won't be returning after the baby is born. Consider this carefully, Ms. Crosby. He isn't exaggerating about the hours."

"No," he said, recovering smoothly. "I never exaggerate."

If I wasn't mistaken, there was a gleam in his eyes, something curious

I wasn't so sure I wanted him to be curious, at all. At least not until I had an answer. *Did he remember me?* Glancing away, I shrugged. "I was being facetious. There's no significant other, male or female." With a vague smile, I looked back at them. "I keep my life uncomplicated. It's far simpler that way. Rest assured, Mr. Gallagher. There is nobody to disappoint."

Especially not myself.

⬤

I HAD A WEEK TO MOVE. The apartment I had wasn't close enough to Gallagher Enterprises, so I was given a temporary residence until something else became available. It's true enough that I hadn't particularly wanted to spend ninety minutes one-way commuting, but I also didn't want to stay in some furnished apartment for an indeterminate amount of time, either.

I wasn't attached to the little condo I had.

There was nothing in Philadelphia I was *attached* to, per se. I didn't *allow* myself to get attached. Not to anything. If you weren't attached to anything—or anyone—it couldn't be taken away.

I had a few friends, but I didn't need to live close to them in order to stay in contact. And those friends were few, indeed. I'd learned to live without attachments. It was no lie when I'd told them I kept my life uncomplicated. It was far simpler than way.

Far, far simpler.

However, as simple as I preferred my life, that residential styled hotel where they had me living for now was a bit more basic than even *I* liked. Gallagher Enterprises had offered me a larger, much more luxurious home, one they offered to visiting executives and I could have used it for a few weeks until I found something more suitable.

Something about living in a home that Drake would pay for rubbed me the wrong way—and he *would* pay for it—it didn't matter if it was him, or his company, in the end, the dollar was his.

I'd convinced them that the hotel would suffice until I found a place of my own, but the four walls of that simple suite-styled hotel were driving me mad. Made me feel trapped, pushing me back to a time I tried hard not to remember.

Finding somewhere else to live was at the top of my list, but I still wouldn't accept their offers of help. Seemed counterproductive when I was here for revenge.

Revenge. Closing my eyes, I pressed my head to the cool glass of the window and wondered. Was I looking for *revenge*?

Or just myself?

Just what did I hope to accomplish here?

I don't fuck naïve little virgins.

Naïve.

Yes. That had been me.

The very first time I'd seen Drake, that summer on the beach, I'd had that whimsical feeling of love of first sight. Seven years older than me, but really, what was seven years, in the scheme of things?

If he'd ignored me, if he'd flirted with the women more his age, if he hadn't been...*kind*...the word hurt, even now...if he hadn't been kind, though, it would have been easier to wipe that schoolgirl crush out of existence.

He still would have destroyed my life.

I still would have lost everything.

The events that unfolded over the coming months *still* would have happened. But would I have drawn into myself so completely? Been so angry?

Perhaps I wouldn't have fancied myself in love with him, wouldn't have spent the course of a summer talking to him, trying to befriend him. Maybe the pain wouldn't have been so devastating, the sense of betrayal so deep.

What-ifs were a waste of time. I *had* befriended him and there was nothing to be done, nothing that would change what had been.

"Befriend him," I muttered, my voice echoing in the silence of the suite. What a laugh. I'd thought he was *lonely*. So I chased after him, the way I tended to do. I talked him into silly, *naïve* little pursuits...fishing, crabbing, swimming. What I couldn't understand was why he'd even bothered to spend any time with me at all.

He'd enjoyed it, I'd thought, at first. Who wouldn't enjoy a lazy swim in the ocean? Or fishing. That was *my* thinking.

Crabbing...well, that was a past time that perhaps wouldn't appeal to everybody, but he'd certainly seemed to enjoy, and he'd definitely had fun enjoying the fruits of our labor.

The afternoons of swimming, though, that had been the best. Followed by an evening just lazing on the beach, the few times he'd allowed himself.

I could still see the way he'd looked coming out of the water, trunks slung low on lean hips, the muscles in his belly rolling as he strode through the waves.

I'd looked at him and wanted.

I'd looked at him and needed.

I'd looked at him and loved. Or so I'd thought. I'd been a foolish girl of seventeen and when you're seventeen, I guess something that turns your heart hot and bright would feel like love. One night, with a fire built on the beach, I'd tried to give myself to him.

Perhaps it was a kindness on his part that had spurred him to speak those cold words.

I don't fuck naïve little virgins.

But kindness wasn't what had pulled his body on top of mine. Kindness hadn't driven him to kiss me, in ways I'd never been kissed before. Kindness wasn't what had guided his hands to untie the bikini top or pull it away and kindness certainly hadn't been the motivating factor when he rolled to his back and let me drag my hands down the hard, muscled wall of his chest.

I was a virgin, yes. Naïve. But so desperate to please.

It wasn't until I'd slid my hand down, tried to touch him that he'd changed.

Naïve little virgins...

Humiliation had driven me away from the beach that night.

I hadn't seen him for another three days.

And when I did see him, everything changed.

He looked at me then with pity in his eyes. Pity, while I sat in the office of the hotel and listened to what my parents had to say. Pity, as I surged up and took off running.

Everything I loved was going to be taken from me.

And he had the nerve to *pity* me, because he'd known all along.

And now he looked at me with no recognition.

There was something else, though. Behind that cool, careful mask, I'd seen it. A glint of hunger, in the depths of those beautiful green eyes.

He'd never act on it, I already knew that.

But it was enough that he wanted.

I wanted to believe that was enough.

Of course, here I was, my overheated face pressed to the cool glass, and I wanted, as well.

Even now, ten years later, I still wanted.

The phone rang, shattering the stillness of the room and I pushed back, turned my head to look at the Samsung HTC that Mai had given me before I'd left the office earlier.

Two days of all the foolishness that new employees had to do. Orientation, security, paperwork. It ate up sixteen hours of my life that I'd never get back.

Tomorrow, I started training with Mai.

And now Drake Gallagher was calling me.

"Hello."

"We have a breakfast meeting at 7:30. Ready for the address?" He didn't say hello.

"Yes." I continued to stare out the window.

He recited the address. I recited it back, not bothering to write it down. My memory was often a curse, but it came in handy, too. "Don't be late," he said.

Then he hung up.

I programmed my alarm, set it 4:30 the following morning. I'd have to get my run in early. If I was going to be around him all day, I needed to get the frustration out sooner rather than later.

I DREAMED OF THE BEACH.

And Drake.

I was seventeen again, and stupid.

The sand was smooth against my back and his hands were rough against my skin as he pulled the bikini top away, palmed one breast. His thumb circled my nipple and excitement, fear, tangled inside me.

His teeth nipped at my neck and I shivered, nervous and needy. As he arched his hips against me, I gasped. His mouth came back to mine. "This is fucking crazy," he whispered, his tongue rasping over my lower lip. His finger and thumb pinched my nipple. "This is insane. I have to..."

I slid a hand down his chest. I knew what he wanted to say and I didn't *want* him to say it. When I felt him through the thin material of his board shorts, I closed my hand around him, stroked. I knew enough to know that guys liked that. Now, he'd stop talking, right?

He rolled to his back, his arms clutching me to him, one hand tangling in my hair while his mouth all but savaged mine. His hips drove up against me and I gasped, felt him between my thighs. The material of his shorts, the denim cut-offs I'd dragged on, they might as well not even exist. Pleasure slammed into me and I cried out, twisting against him just to feel it once more. I could feel myself, slick and needy, the material of my bikini bottom slipping against my flesh as I moved.

"Shan..." he muttered.

It was that sound that woke me.

The sound of his voice.

Sucking in oxygen, trying to calm the need raging inside me, I closed my eyes and drove my head back against the pillow. Of *course* I'd wake up...in just that moment.

Of all the dreams I had, of all the nightmares that held me trapped, I had to wake up from that one. I'd been enjoying it.

"Why?" I muttered, flinging my forearm across my eyes and blowing out a breath while I lay there, my heart racing.

My breasts throbbed, tingled, pulsing in time with the need that all but wrenched through my cunt.

Groaning, I rolled onto my belly and shoved my face into the pillow.

If I thought it would do me any good, I would have slid my hand down, brought the climax that seemed to dance just out of reach.

It was a lie, though.

The first, and only, orgasm I'd had was that night on the beach, as Drake dragged me back and forth against his cock.

I'd tried to recreate it, capture that amazing moment. When it seemed like my skin had dissolved and my soul tried to escape, while his mouth ate at mine and his body was the only thing that kept me anchored to this world.

But it eluded me. The more frustrated I became, the harder it was to climax and the harder it was, the more frustrated I became.

The frustration had bled over onto every relationship, tainted the way I saw every man. It didn't help that there were...shadows. Other things that bled into my life and kept me from letting myself connect the way I could have, the way I'd wanted to.

Even now, the shadows of my past with Drake were creeping up on me. Keeping me awake, burning. *Yearning.*

"You have to stop this," I whispered. "You need to sleep."

For nearly two years, I'd visited a therapist after my father's murder. I couldn't sleep and when I could, I'd been plagued by nightmares. There were tricks she'd taught me, ways to coax my mind into relaxing and if I ever I needed to do that, it was now.

I had to sleep, because if I wanted to be on my toes around him, I couldn't afford to be tired.

Forcing him out of my mind, I thought back to the beach. Before him. The waves crashing against the sand, the sound of the water. I'd always loved the sound of the water...

Cool blue light surrounded me.

Blue light. Water.

Blue light...

The moments between wakefulness and dreams can be such fickle things.

One moment I was concentrating.

The next, I was in the dark and there was no blue light, no soothing crash of the waves on the ocean.

There was just fear.

Cruel hands.

A fist in my hair as I was dragged up.

"Get up."

My father's voice. "Please don't. I'll—"

The words were cut off as a fist slammed into his face. My mother's scream.

The clock went off.

And I was no longer in the bed. At some point, during the nightmare that had come and gone in a blink, and yet lasted forever,

I'd climbed out of bed and hidden myself in the corner. With my knees clutched to my chest and my hair damp and sweaty in my eyes, I sat there, shaking, half sick.

The alarm continued to echo through my room, *Daughtry's* HOME. But I couldn't work up the energy to get up and move.

Not yet.

Not yet.

———◆———

THE SUIT I CHOSE TO wear was another one in gray, this one a soft dove gray that almost matched my eyes. My muscles felt relaxed, loose from my standard, early morning run but the dregs of the nightmare still clung. The sound of the phone had me jumping and I almost spilled my coffee when I reached for it.

"Get a grip," I said, straightening the cup as I checked the phone. It was just after six. Too early for ringing phones, unless it was a coffee fairy promising me that a latte with a double shot of espresso was just outside the door. I was on my third cup of coffee and the cobwebs were still muddling my thoughts.

"I'm sending a car around. Are you ready?"

I frowned. "I have the address. I can simply drive."

"We have other business to attend to after. It's simpler to have a car pick you up," he said. "Are you ready?"

I looked down at my bare feet. "I will be in a few moments. When can I expect the car?"

"Five minutes."

Five minutes, I mouthed, lowering the phone to stare at it for a moment. Was he trying to catch me off-guard? "I'll be ready."

Without another cup of coffee, perhaps, but I could be ready.

A pair of heels a shade darker than my suit waited by my bed. I stepped into them, checked my appearance.

Then I grabbed my purse, looked at my watch. Three minutes. If I hurried, I could maybe grab a cup of coffee on the way out the door.

The hallway was quiet, just a few sleepy-eyed travelers coming out of their rooms, rolling suitcases in tow, purses or briefcases in hand. A few carried suit bags. There were seven of us waiting at the elevator bank and I shot another sidelong look at my watch as the doors slid open. Two minutes. Normally, I wouldn't be concerned about a minute here or there, but I had the oddest feeling I was being tested here. That, coupled with the night I had, left me feeling on edge.

I slid off the elevator with fifteen seconds remaining on my five-minute window. No time for coffee. I strode out the door with just a brief nod at the woman who stood behind the welcome desk, everything in me longing for more coffee. I needed that jolt like I needed air.

No time for breakfast, either. It didn't matter that I'd been told this was a breakfast meeting. I was an assistant. If personal experience was anything to go by, then I might be lucky if I had a chance to grab a cup of coffee when the meeting was over. I could have done just fine without food, but I was about ready to hurt somebody over the fact that I hadn't had a chance to have another cup of coffee.

The cool morning air closed around me and I breathed it in, let it soothe some of the ragged edges away as I turned my head, looking for the car—there.

It was that one. I didn't even have to wait for it to roll to a stop a few inches away from the curb where I stood.

It was steel gray.

It seemed to be the color Gallagher preferred. I needed to update my wardrobe. Anything but gray.

The driver's door swung open but before he could climb out, the door nearest me opened and I found myself looking in at the man himself. "It's okay, Jake. We need to get moving."

I eyed him narrowly, kept the smooth expression on my face as I slid into the car. I was glad I'd worn a skirt with a fuller cut. It made it easier to shift and situate without the potential for embarrassment. I fumbled a bit with my bag and the door, but managed to get the door to close behind me as I settled on the seat next to him. A familiar scent, rich and intoxicating, filled the air around me. Coffee. I might have let myself drool, if I dared. Had it been anybody but Gallagher, I would have.

"Right on time. You're very efficient," he said, his voice pensive.

"I'd think that would be a good quality in an assistant." I held his gaze and that alone had the dregs of the nightmare falling away. Too bad I was left to shift uncomfortably with the memory of the *other* dream swimming to the front of my mind. Sitting there, I tried not to remember *that* dream, where his body hovered over mine, the sand warm against my back, those green eyes boring into mine. My belly went hot, my skin felt tight and my palms started to sweat. Those thoughts were the absolute last things I could hold in my mind when I was here with him.

"Of course," he murmured. Then he looked away, dismissing me.

It took a moment to recall what we'd been discussing.

It took even longer to get my foolish body under control.

Needing something to think about besides the coffee he held in his hand, I composed my face into the professional mask that was going to be the only part of me I ever let him see. Looking around, I saw nobody else, save for the driver in the front seat. It was just the two of us.

"Are we picking Mai up as well?"

"Yes." He continued to watch me, and a glint in those eyes bothered me. It bothered me a lot, but looking away was a sign of discomfort. Worse, a sign of nervousness and I wasn't going to let him see that he made me nervous—I wouldn't *let* myself be nervous.

Arrogant son of a bitch.

A moment later, that hard mouth softened as a smile appeared and he shook his head, like he was amused by some personal, private joke. *What? Why are you laughing?*

He looked away and I let myself do the same while thoughts spun dizzyingly through my mind. The past few days, I'd spent hours comparing myself to the girl I'd been, the silly child he'd known. The girl from which he'd taken everything.

Nothing of her remained.

She'd been soft and happy and foolish.

There was nothing soft about me; while I might have bits and pieces of my life that made me happy, I allowed it only in small doses. Happiness was something I didn't trust.

It was a lie. An illusion and nothing I'd ever trust in again.

The drive passed in silence and I had to fight the urge to breathe out a sigh of relief as we pulled up in front of a pretty, old building. Ivy clung to the front, and even in the dim light of morning, I could see the vivid bursts of flowers in the window boxes. A little bit of color on a drab morning. Unaware that I was smiling, I leaned my head against the door, studying the building. It suited Mai. Old-world elegance and beauty.

"You're smiling."

I turned my head, stared at Gallagher who sat a little closer than I liked. I glanced at the coffee he held, a wistful bit of envy curling curl inside me. I wanted that damn coffee. "Was I?" I asked, focusing my attention away from him.

"Yes. Mai and her husband will be moving out of the city after the baby is born. They want a larger home. If you like the building, I can see if anybody has inquired about her unit."

"No, thank you. It's lovely, but it's not my style." I had to coax the disinterest into my voice. It was lovely. But I had no desire to accept any help from him. I had the job. I had a goal. The goal was still murky—I wanted...what, exactly?

"Not your style. Just what is your style, Shan...non?"

Was it me, or had he lingered on the way he drew out my name?

My breath caught and his gaze dropped, briefly, to linger on my mouth. Blood heated my neck, my cheeks and I was lucky that at that very moment, the driver slid out of the car. "There she is, sir. I'll get her settled and we can get on the road. Traffic isn't too terrible today."

Saved, I thought, by the arrival of Mai. She glided toward us, elegant and beautiful in a simple black sheath, the hard mound of her belly not terribly obvious until she turned to shift into the car. A soft groan escaped her as she settled into the front seat, next to the driver. She glanced back at us. "I have to be up front," she said, smiling, although she looked tired. "I've got this annoying habit of getting nauseated if I'm in the back. How are you doing, Shannon?"

"Well enough. Good morning, Mai," I murmured. She had a clever hand with makeup, but she hadn't slept well, either.

Gallagher was less polite. "You're not sleeping well anymore."

"It's getting harder *to* sleep," she said, an edge I hadn't heard before creeping into her voice. "Any idea what it's like to sleep when you have a foot driving into your kidney?"

He blinked. "No. I can't say I'm familiar with that."

She sighed, leaning her head back against the seat. "Trust me. It isn't pleasant."

"If you need to go home and rest..."

Mai shook her head. "No. And I want to make sure Shannon is comfortable with her position before I leave." An amused grin lit her face as she glanced back at us. "After all, it's not like I plan on coming back to help out."

He looked as though he wanted to argue, but she just shook her head. "I'll leave when I'm ready—or when the baby is. Until then, please let me do my job. I think I might actually miss it when I'm gone."

THE VIRGIN

THE MEETING WAS TO discuss a possible acquisition.

Gallagher Enterprises had started as a small architectural firm located in Buffalo, NY. That was thirty years ago. Now there were offices in Philadelphia, New York, Orlando and Los Angeles, each of them headed by one of the Gallagher sons. Drake's father, Seamus Gallagher, had retired seven years ago and the company just continued to grow and grow. His boys knew what they were doing; I had to give them credit.

They were looking to acquire a foundering architectural firm in the Dallas area and the man currently blustering with Gallagher was out of his league. He also had roaming eyes, a loud, fake laugh and hands that squeezed just a bit too tight. He liked to invade personal space, too. Particularly mine.

He also liked to call me *honey*, although I'd introduced myself and corrected him twice.

I was torn between ignoring him and addressing the issue.

As I passed out notepads to everybody, he reached up, patted me on the back, just a little too low to be comfortable, but too high for me to claim he'd actually grabbed my ass. Quickly moving out of his reach, I inclined my head. "Is there anything you need, Mr. Paxton?"

"Honey, I need a refill on my coffee." He winked at me. "You just keep this good and topped off and we'll get along fine."

"Shannon." Gallagher gave me a narrow look and nodded at the seat next to him.

I inclined my head and made my way around the table. A huge breakfast buffet spread out behind us, servers at the ready. One was already moving toward Paxton with coffee. Asshole.

"Shannon is my admin, Ken." Gallagher gave him a smile. It was polite, to the point of being *too* polite. "She's not here to top off your coffee. She's here to help facilitate the meeting and assist me. If you need coffee, just let one of the servers know. I'm sure they'd be happy to help."

Paxton opened his mouth, his face going a slow, ugly red. Then he blinked, nodded. "Absolutely. My apologies, honey."

I had to fight not to grit my teeth as I pulled out my tablet and pulled up the necessary files. Mai had already told me what information Gallagher might need, but she'd also let me know that most of the time I'd just need to make notes, observations. *He researches everything and while he might use you and the team to gather the information, he's involved in every project that interests him, from the ground up.*

I didn't take that to mean I wasn't going to be needed.

However, if he actually wanted to work with somebody like Paxton, my opinion of him was going to drop and it was already not terribly high. Paxton was an ass, and he wouldn't treat his employees well. Personally, I had issues with Gallagher. On a professional level, he seemed to make his people happy.

Paxton was his polar opposite.

That meeting dragged on for what seemed like hours.

In reality, it was only 117 minutes. I counted them, each and every one. It was excruciating, sitting there next to him, smelling the light, subtle cologne he used—or maybe it was just his soap, I couldn't tell. Every so often, he'd shift in his seat, leaning on the arm until he was close enough that I could feel his body heat and I'd have to grit my teeth until I could subtly shift my position away from him.

A tension headache had settled at the base of my skull by the time it was over and once everybody rose, I was glad to have a chance to rise, stretch my muscles. Mai glanced at me. "Before we hit the road, I'm taking a quick break. Join me?"

Code speak for wanna hit the ladies room.

I nodded and gathered my things, tucked them into the soft, eggplant-colored bag I'd picked up a few days ago. Slinging the strap over my shoulder, I fell in beside her as we wove through the bodies. People were speaking in low tones, all except for Paxton. That big, booming voice carried across the room as he said, "Now, Drake, you let me know if there's anything else we can help you with. I think we'd make a fine addition to the Gallagher family."

I managed to keep my face straight as I ducked out of the room.

The cool peace of the ladies room closed around us and I let myself breathe a quiet sigh of relief.

Mai shot me a wide grin. "And here I was thinking that was *my* line."

"Three cups of coffee," I lied, making a beeline for the nearest stall.

She chuckled and went to do the same.

The sound of her heels stopped just before I reached the door and I paused, looked back at her.

She was staring down at the floor, a dismayed look on her face. "Oh. I think I just...how embarrassing."

A funny feeling settled in the pit of my gut. It only spread as she reached up and settled a hand on her belly.

"Oh, no," she whispered. "Shannon, I think I've got a bit of a problem. I think my water just broke."

Her eyes were dazed, confused as she looked up at me. "I've still got a month. How can that happen?"

The demanding pang in my bladder subsided as I moved back to her side. "Well, like you said earlier. You'll leave when the baby is ready. I think the baby just decided he was ready."

"She." She swallowed and went back to staring at the puddle on the floor. "The baby is a girl."

I reached for my phone. "Come on. Let's get to the door and we'll call..."

"Drake. Call Drake. He'll get me to the hospital and I can call my husband on the drive."

"Drake, then."

"I'm sorry, Shannon." Her voice was thin and soft as she squeezed my hand. "I wanted to make sure you were okay before this happened."

Gallagher's voice came on the line. "We need to get going, Shannon."

"We have an...issue," I said. It wasn't a problem, really. The baby had just moved up the timetable, right?

Chapter Three

TWO WEEKS INTO MY JOB.

I lay face-down on my bed and decided this was the best way ever to make sure I was cured of any sort of romantic inclinations.

When I thought about Drake Gallagher these days, I mostly wanted to have a picture of him thumbtacked to my wall so I could throw darts at his perfect face.

My shoes, the cute pair of Jimmy Choos I'd bought as a treat for myself, and wore only when I needed a pick-me-up, were still on my feet and I hated them. Kicking them off, I rolled onto my back and stared up at the ceiling. There wasn't a bone in my body that didn't hurt.

My eyes were gritty from lack of sleep. He was indeed in the office most days by seven. I was ready to leave my room by six thirty, because I didn't trust him to not pull another stunt like he had the day of the breakfast meeting.

He usually worked until seven or later. Typically, I took a sandwich with me, but ended up eating on the go and that morning, a skirt that had previously fit me like a glove had fit a little loose in the waist.

I wasn't eating right and I couldn't sleep. The nightmares had returned with a vengeance; stress brought them on and I was most certainly stressed.

This job sucked and I still wasn't certain just why I was doing this.

He didn't remember me.

I don't fuck naïve little virgins.

Of course he didn't. With a job like this, he probably didn't even have time to masturbate.

Grimacing, I sat up and stared morosely around the bland, beige-painted walls of the hotel room. I hadn't even had time to look for a place to stay, although that was on the calendar for tomorrow. He was working from nine until noon, cutting off at noon sharp and I had to remind him because he had an important personal matter.

And then I had freedom. Maybe even thirty-six hours of it.

Mai had offered to contact a real estate agent she knew. Gallagher had all but tried to push several places into my lap. But he owned those buildings. I wanted my own place—ideally, something he didn't own. And most importantly of all, he wasn't going to pick it out for me.

I curled my tired toes, then stretched my feet and stood up. "I'll start looking," I murmured. After I sat in the tub for a little while. Or maybe *while* I sat in the tub.

That, actually, seemed to be the ideal solution.

Wine, my tablet, a hot tub of water, and I could get a jump on this looking thing. I already knew the general area I needed to look in. Mai was in the right area. Residential, quiet. Probably a little pricier than I wanted, but as long as I was working for Gallagher, I could afford it without even touching the money I had in the bank. Her building, while lovely, wasn't ultimately what I wanted, even though he had nudged me toward it, several times.

I wanted something simpler, plainer. Someplace I wouldn't fall in love with. Something that would never feel like home.

I hadn't had a home since I'd been forced to leave mine.

I preferred to keep the status quo.

While the water was running, I went to get my wine, settling on a nice, sweet red. Business dinners were a chore for me. They served wines that left me feeling like I'd shoved a barrel full of crackers into my mouth, reds that were too dry left a horrible aftertaste. The only wines I enjoyed were the sweeter ones, and the sweeter, the better. There was a lovely ice wine waiting in the refrigerator for me, but I'd save that for a really bad day. Today had sucked, but it was a seven on the suckage scale. I'd wait until I hit a nine before I broke open the ice wine.

In under ten minutes, I was in water almost up to my chin, a glass of wine on the side of the tub, with my tablet tucked inside a protective case while I skimmed the local ads for an available apartment.

Too big.

Too little.

Too pricy.

The price was right, but from what I could tell about the pictures, it was ugly. I didn't want a *home*, but I wanted to be comfortable.

More of the same...

Thirty minutes later, my glass of wine was empty and the water was cold, and I hadn't narrowed anything down.

I finished up in the bath, dried off and changed into a loose pair of pajama bottoms and a tank top, leaving my hair to air dry. I debated on heading in to bed, but decided I needed one more glass of wine. This was the closest to relaxed I'd felt in weeks, ever since I'd seen the job opening.

With my wine in one hand, the tablet in another, I settled on the miniscule balcony.

But I didn't start looking again.

From my position, I could see the sleek ivory and glass tower of Gallagher Enterprises. Was he still there?

He had told me to leave a little before eight, when the phone had rang. I'd finished up, and done just that as he took the call. Who was I to argue with the boss?

A smirk curved my lips and I tipped my glass toward the tower. "Here's to two weeks."

I didn't know how long I'd make it.

So far, I hadn't fucked anything up terribly bad, but this wasn't a job I'd want for life.

I just wanted...

Closing my eyes, I lifted my glass to my lips.

Perhaps it was having the wine inside me, and next to no food. I hadn't had dinner. Lunch had been half of the sandwich I'd packed and nothing else. Breakfast had been a Powerbar and a latte on the way down the elevator.

The wine made it easier to be honest and I really let myself acknowledge *why* I was doing this.

I wanted Drake Gallagher. One time.

Just once.

I wanted what he'd teased me with all those years ago, before he'd pulled away and so coolly dismissed me.

And I wanted to see the hunger in *his* eyes.

Some petty part of me wanted to find a way to destroy him, as he'd destroyed me. I was in a position to do that, perhaps. But corporate espionage or anything else that truly *could* destroy him, that was nothing I would stoop to.

I'd settle for seeing the want reflected in his eyes. I'd like to make him burn for me. Long for me. Ache for me. I'd like to make myself an addiction in his blood, like he'd been in mine all this time.

Then I'd satisfy that need, once. Only once, before I walked away. Maybe once I did that, I could be...normal. Have those relationships that women my age were supposed to have. Have a foolish fling, find a guy, fall in love. Just be *normal*.

But first I had to break through the wall that had been built that summer. If I had the chance.

Somehow, I didn't see it happening.

Perhaps there had been a time or two when I'd caught him watching me, when he didn't realize I could see him.

It was nothing he would act on, though. Interest wasn't madness.

And it needed to be madness.

"I've enough madness for both of us," I murmured.

I continued to sip the wine and brood, my eyes still on the tower.

THE VIRGIN

THE RINGING OF THE phone woke me.

I came awake, offguard and cold. The temperature had dropped and I'd fallen asleep on the balcony. Shivering as I searched for the phone, I spied it on the table through the open door. I reached it just before it would have rolled to voicemail.

If that dragon was trying to call me into work *now*—

"Yes." I'd tried to keep my voice cool, so I didn't snap. I made it downright cold instead and winced at the sound of it.

There was a pause. Then Gallagher asked, "Am I interrupting?"

"Hardly. I was almost asleep. How may I help you, sir?"

"I was just calling to let you know not to come in tomorrow."

"Of course. Feel free to text me any time your needs change." I grabbed a pen from the table and gouged it toward my belly. I needed to learn to watch my mouth. Already realizing this wasn't going as I'd planned, I considered making him fire me. If he had to go through the hell of finding another assistant...

"I prefer talking when possible. Voices are much more pleasant than words on a screen. Get some sleep, Shannon. You sound like you need it."

Making a face at the phone, I waited until I hung up before I muttered, "Thank you for your permission."

WAS IT A GOOD SIGN that I found an acceptable apartment within the first two hours?

There was even an agent available. Now that was luck beyond belief. I was able to do a walk-through, ask all the questions I needed to ask—they wanted a six-month commitment and that hurt, but even if things didn't work out with Gallagher, this was a price I could afford for six months, should I need to stay in Philadelphia. First and last month's rent, standard. A security check as well, which wasn't an issue.

The only question was did I want it.

No.

The apartment I wanted was actually a street down from Mai's, a charming little place with a rooftop garden, a window seat where I could curl up and read and daydream. But it could too easily become home.

Turning in the middle of the stark white kitchen with its polished chrome appliances and shiny black accents, I looked at the agent. "I'll take it."

It was boring. It was sterile. In short, it was perfect for what I needed.

A place to sleep, eat and shower while I decided just how I was going to proceed, if I was going to proceed, and how to back out of this if I decided I was just done.

My phone rang.

Looking down, I saw a familiar name on the screen.

A knot settled in my throat.

I hadn't lied...exactly...when I said there was no family who would be disappointed if I worked long hours.

My mother understood. I buried myself in school after we'd left Massachusetts, and then I'd buried myself in work.

But she wouldn't understand this.

Sighing, I answered the call as I headed down the sidewalk, not sparing a glance at the apartment that would be mine within days. "Hi, Mom."

"Shan...how are you, baby?"

"Crazy busy. How are you and Paul?"

"Wonderful. We're taking a trip to Martinique this fall. If you can get the time off, you should come. Paul would love to spend more time with you."

"That's sweet, Mom. But I just started a new job. It will be a while before I get any vacation time. I do get a few days off at Christmas, so I'll be sure to come to Virginia and visit then, okay?" Mom had settled in Virginia five years earlier and not long after, she'd met Paul, a retired OB/GYN. Not exactly the romantic sort I'd have gone chasing after, but he adored my mom and he made her happy. After the hand life had dealt her, Mom deserved happy. She loved him, his quiet, steady ways, the gentle humor. He took care of her and after a lifetime of trying to keep up with a dreamer like my father, she deserved to have somebody take care of her for a change.

"Why am I not surprised to hear this?" Mom sighed, good-naturedly. "Okay, tell me about the new job."

I did, giving her a skeletal outline that didn't include the name of the company, my boss, or anything that might give me away. "He works me to death, but the pay is wonderful. I might buy another pair of Jimmy Choos in a week."

"Considering how much you're on your feet, you should get something more comfortable," Mom said.

"They are very comfortable." I shrugged absently as I wandered down the street, finding myself in a little shopping area. It would be nice, having something like this close to home. A gift display caught my eye. A baby gift—a pretty little pink sleeper, paired with bibs, some sort of cloth and a stack of diapers. I thought of Mai and headed into the store. "I just spend too much time on my feet. After that many hours, nothing is comfortable."

"True enough."

We chatted a few more minutes while I eyed the gifts and then Mom sighed. "Paul is waving me down. He bought a new grill and he's experimenting with recipes every other day. Sometimes, it's bliss. Other days, my belly wants to hide. I think it'll want to hide today. I have to go, baby. I love you."

"Love you, too, Mom."

"Buy something pretty for your new place, honey. You never settle in anywhere."

I made an assenting sound under my breath, knowing that if I said anything I'd either lie, or worry her.

Once the call disconnected, I turned and looked at the lady behind the counter. "I'd like something like what you have displayed in the window, please."

<hr>

"IT'S LOVELY." MAI BEAMED over the sleeper, although it looked almost identical to the one her little girl wore.

"I have the receipt if you'd like to exchange it."

"No. I adore it. It was so kind of you to the take the time on your day off. I know you are probably enjoying having a little time to yourself."

I rolled my eyes before I could stop myself. "True enough."

Mai laughed. "Please. I know how Drake is."

"He did warn me." I gave her a polite smile and focused on the baby I held. She smelled sweet. That warm baby smell that was unique to infants. "She's so precious."

"I know." Mai sighed happily and then shifted her dark eyes back to me.

That penetrating stare had me fighting the urge to shift uncomfortably on the seat. Instead, I just cocked a brow. "Yes?"

"I watched you, you know."

"Your job was to get me trained."

She waved a hand. "Before that. The day of the interview. Remember Ms. Simone?"

Hmmmm. Tricky ground. "Vaguely."

Mai wagged a finger. "Liar. You can probably describe what she was wearing. In detail. Man, I'd kill to have legs like hers."

"You've got a better attitude."

A bright laugh escaped her and the baby in my arms jolted a little, her eyes flying wide before she settled back against me. "Oh, who doesn't? You know why she wasn't hired, don't you?" She leaned back, sighing a little, as elegant in her jeans and t-shirt as she'd been in her suits and dresses. "Her resume was as impressive as yours was. I'll admit, I was pushing Drake to hiring her. Until that little *There is absolutely nothing I'm incapable of, Mr. Gallagher*...bit. You know what she was getting at. You're not stupid; I'm not."

I shrugged. "Maybe she was just enthusiastic and it came out wrong."

"Bullshit." She leaned forward now, her eyes shrewd. "He doesn't mix sex with business. Ever. But he watches you. I'm not going to lie and say he's never shown any sign of interest in the women he's worked with, but he doesn't mix the two. He'll keep his interest to just that and he rarely lets the interest show, so it's weird that I caught it."

Something hot twisted inside me. It wasn't hope. It couldn't be that. Yeah, I *hoped* he would want me and if I could play that, I would. But that hot, flighty little feeling was too much for hoping he might want to fuck me. And that was all I wanted, all I could want. Nerves? Could it be nerves?

Mai continued to watch me, her eyes unreadable. "Nothing to say?"

With a careless shrug, I managed, finally, to form words. "I'm not sure what you're seeing, because I haven't seen it. Regardless, I'm just looking to do my job." *Liar, liar, pants on fire*!

But I'd become very skilled at lying, so skilled she just looked at me and nodded, believing every word I said.

"I get that," she said softly. "I'm just warning you. If he...well. Just be aware. Even if he acts interested, don't return it. Not if you want to keep the job. It's a good job, but if anything personal arises, you'll be done at the company, and he doesn't do commitment. I don't think he even does repeat dates."

"That isn't surprising." I shifted the baby to my shoulder and busied myself with looking down at her. "Don't worry, Mai. Like I said, I'm here for a job. My career is the most important thing my life."

She watched me, her eyes wise, almost too wise.
Something told me she didn't believe me.
But she didn't argue with me, either.

Chapter Four

MOVING SUCKS.

Even when you don't own a lot, and the movers are handling most of it for you; moving still sucks.

My back ached from moving boxes from one room to the other, my thighs felt like rubber and my feet hurt.

Of course, any more, my feet *always* hurt, but this was the weekend, two o'clock on a Sunday and my feet should be getting a break. Instead, I was still carting boxes around.

The ringing of the doorbell didn't put me in a better frame of mind and I almost ignored it, but a lifetime of having manners drilled into me kept me from doing that.

Those manners almost failed me as I saw who stood on the other side.

What in the hell...

Sighing, I undid the chain and opened it to see Gallagher standing there. Sweat trickled down my brow and I swiped it aside as I said, "Mr. Gallagher. I didn't overlook a meeting, did I?" I knew I hadn't. I'd synced the calendars and double-checked everything before I left yesterday at one.

"No. I was at Mai's yesterday. She told me you were moving this weekend. I came by to see if you needed help."

He came inside without waiting for an invitation and I huffed out a sigh, staring at his back. He wore a black t-shirt, one that stretched over hard muscles. It hung out, untucked, over his jeans. Faded jeans. Perfectly faded and they clung to long, lean thighs. Bastard. Why did he have to look so good? "You should have just called. Everything is under control. It's not your job to help me settle in."

He turned and looked at me, a grin crooking his lips in a way that was actually rather adorable, if I'd let myself *think* of him as adorable. But I couldn't do that. Already my belly felt hot and tight and I wanted to run my hands through his hair. Soft, gleaming darkly red under the lights. "Of course it's not my job. It's called being friendly, Shannon," he said softly.

"It's unnecessary."

He tucked his hands into his back pockets, eying me. "So you're all unpacked, then."

"No." I frowned at him.

"Then I can help." He turned and moved deeper into the apartment. "This...isn't what I would have seen you choosing. There was something open near Mai's. Did you see it?"

"I saw it. This suits my needs." I floundered for some reason to throw him out, but what in the hell was I going to say? *You can't stay here? I'm dirty and I'm cranky and I'm not wearing a bra and I can't look at you without wanting you?*

That wasn't going to go over well.

He tossed a look over his shoulder. "It suits your needs? What about what you want?"

My belly twisted, hot and demanding. What I *wanted* stood right in front of me. Reaching for it was a different matter altogether.

Turning away from him, I strode over to the refrigerator and opened it. "This is what I want. Otherwise, I wouldn't have taken it. Would you like a bottle of water?"

"No. I'm good. So...where do you want me?"

He stood only five feet in front of the bedroom door. The mattress was still stripped, but who needed sheets?

I jerked my chin into the living room. "I need to get my books unpacked, as well as the dishes."

THE VIRGIN

ONCE HE WAS IMMERSED in the books, I ducked into my bedroom and shut the door. Whipping off my shirt, I pulled on the bra I'd stripped off earlier and then hurriedly dressed once more. Because I didn't want to risk having him offer to help in here, I took care of the few boxes that remained. Mostly it was sheets and bedding, a picture of my mom which I tucked into a drawer for now. I had changed a great deal in ten years.

She hadn't.

That taken care of, I looked around. The majority of it was done, save for my clothes. That could always be done later.

It took roughly twenty minutes to get the bedroom settled and then I opened the door to find he had finished one box and was working on another. He glanced up at me. His gaze lingered on me just a little too long and heat crept up my neck, along my skin, until I thought about walking back over to the refrigerator and opening the door just to cool myself off. "You don't have a lot to unpack," he said, turning back to the books he was shelving. He kept them in the same order I'd boxed them in. Considerate. "Is there more in storage?"

"No. This is all I have, Mr. Gallagher."

He frowned at me. "You can call me Drake."

"I prefer not to, sir."

He paused, one hand lingering on the spine of a book before stroking down it. "Any reason for that, Shannon?" he asked, his voice soft, an odd tone in it. He did it again, too. Lingering on the second syllable of my name.

When I didn't answer, he turned his head, looked at me.

There was a look there, in the back of his eyes. My breath hitched in my lungs. I wondered. Had to wonder.

Did he remember? If he did, he'd say it. Now, if ever, there was a time. We weren't at the office and this was the perfect time.

"Is it a professionalism thing or you just don't much care for me?"

In my heart, a crack that I hadn't realized was still there widened, split even further. No. He didn't remember.

Sighing, I moved back into the kitchen and reached for the box opener, cut open another box. "I simply prefer to address my bosses by their surnames. As to whether or not I care for you, you are my boss. My personal feelings aren't an issue."

The one time my feelings *had* been an issue for me, they hadn't mattered to him, at all.

Why was he concerned about them now?

"YOU'VE GOT TO BE THE most tidy, efficient person I've ever come across."

It took less than two hours. When he realized that all I had left were the towels and my clothes, he took the box of towels and spare sheets and gestured to the bedroom. "You'll be busy all week and you'll sleep better if you know you're unpacked," he said, giving me a narrow look. "If you're this organized, it's in your nature. So unpack the clothes. I'll handle the towels."

"They are my towels." I was tempted to insist, but at that point, I really wanted a long, hot soak—one thing this place did have that I had coveted was a Jacuzzi tub and I was going to soak until I turned into a prune. It would be easier if I didn't have to unearth all the towels. "Fine. If you insist, the bathroom is through here."

I turned my back on him so I didn't have the sight of him in my bedroom imprinted on my memory and then I busied myself with hauling my suit bags and the suitcases out of the closet. Two dozen suits made up the majority of my wardrobe and most of them would have to be ironed. Oh, the fun we'll have... I blew out a sigh and thought maybe the long bath wouldn't be as long as I'd like.

"Nice tub."

I jumped and spun around to see him in the doorway, the empty box hanging from one big, long-fingered hand. "Yes." And damn him, now I had the image of him in my bedroom, standing just there in the doorway with the decadent bathroom at his back, the black t-shirt stretched across his flat belly, over wide shoulders.

My mouth went dry and my heart started to hammer within my chest.

Not the images I needed in my head. Turning back to the closet, I straightened out the suits I'd just hung up and turned to the bed to get another handful.

He was already there, holding the remaining suits. I stepped aside as he came my way. I wasn't going to have a wrestling contest over the damn suits. That meant I might have to *touch* him. Then I'd have that memory in me as well.

"What else?"

What other memories?

I swallowed and headed over to the bed. "Everything else is personal. Which I can handle easily enough on my own. Thank you for your help, sir."

"Are you hungry?"

"Hungry?" I frowned and looked up.

"Yeah. You haven't done any shopping—I saw the fridge. I know the neighborhood. Mai isn't far from here. There's a great pizza place. Are you hungry?"

My belly rumbled, as if on cue.

His gaze dropped, lingered on my midsection, a grin curling on his lips. Sighing, I turned away. "Do you really have nothing else to do with your time, Mr. Gallagher?"

"Oh, I can think of plenty I should do. But I decided I wanted to do this. Now I want pizza. I'm going to get some either way. The question is, do you want to share it with me or not?"

Damn him. Now I wanted pizza, too.

And what was I going to do, keep pushing him back until I figured out just what I was here to *do*?

It sure as hell wasn't because I *liked* having him work me into the ground.

"Pizza sounds fine," I said, staring at the blindingly white wall in front of me.

Dinner. It would just be dinner. I could maybe convince myself to relax.

Mai had said he watched me and twice today I'd noticed him doing just that.

Maybe, just maybe, I could figure out where to go from here.

———◉———

OR MAYBE *not*.

He made easy small talk, ate nearly three fourths of a large pie and then left.

As his footsteps faded down the hall, I leaned my back against the door and closed my eyes.

Then, because I was too tired just then do anything else, I locked the door, trudged down the hall and collapsed face first on the bed.

I seemed to spend a lot of time in this position ever since I'd started my little...experiment.

"I'm a glutton for punishment," I mumbled into the bed.

An afternoon around a man I wanted like I wanted to breathe. Maybe more. I knew what it was like to breathe, and while breathing was *necessary*, I knew what breathing was like. I actually *craved* him, but I had no idea what it would be like.

Actually, I had no idea what sex would be like, period.

I'd closed down after that summer. Even when the pain faded, even when the sense of betrayal no longer cut so deep, there had been a sense of...grief. All of it was tied together in my mind, forged into a chain by that grief, by my own misery and obsession and a wall had begun to form.

That wall closed me off and I couldn't scale it, no matter how hard I tried. For the longest time, I hadn't *wanted* to. When the grief and the guilt finally started to fade, the mad crept in.

It wasn't until my senior year of college that I finally let it all go enough to try to start living again. Doug. Doug Anderson had driven me a mild form of crazy and if it hadn't been for one minor detail, I might have actually slept *tried* to sleep with him. Maybe he could have helped me climb that wall. I don't know. I'd *wanted* to. I'd wanted him.

He'd brought me so close...so very close, close enough that the hunger I'd felt for him had kept me lying awake more than once.

He had a way with his hands, a way with his mouth. A way with everything, really.

I'd kept quiet about a number of things in school. My past, the shadows that I'd tried to outrun. And he'd had some secrets of his own. Including a lover that he was still in love with.

I could understand, really. I knew what it was like to want somebody.

But his lover, a sexy, worthless bastard who really didn't deserve him, made a repeat appearance in his life. Doug was bisexual—that was the secret he'd kept from me. I didn't *care* about his sexuality. I did care about the fact that he'd been using me to try to forget about the guy he was still in love with.

He was sorry, of course. He did care for me, and he was sorry he'd hurt me.

Could we be friends?

We could.

We still were.

But it was another nail in my virginal coffin.

The two men who I'd thought were the ones had so *not* been.

I didn't give up *right* away. There were a few other guys I dated in college, but the first guy was one who'd heard about Doug's...alternative sexuality and he'd been convinced that meant I must be desperate for a good lay. He'd actually *told* me that. There was no way I was going to waste another minute with him. I'd left him in the middle of the meal after tossing down a ten to pay for my burger. The next guy had been pre-med and he wanted a list of the guys I'd been with before he would even *kiss* me.

I'd decided to focus on college.

And nights passed while I dreamt about Drake.

Not too much time went by without me thinking about him. In fits of rage, yes. But often with just...longing. Need. I'd wanted him, even at seventeen, more than I'd wanted anybody else, after him.

It wasn't until two years ago that I realized the truth of it, until I understood why I felt closed off. That was when I began to understand the truth about the wall inside me. Until I had him out of my system, I'd never have a *real* chance with somebody else. That was when I'd started looking. Watching.

I'd had a chance to move to Philadelphia—he headed up the offices here, something I was well aware of—I'd taken it, knowing that I was putting myself closer and closer.

It had taken all this time to get *here*.

Part of me wondered if I shouldn't just go up to him and say...something.

You broke my heart, ruined my family when I was a kid. Now I'm a sexual screw-up and I think it's your fault. Why don't we have sex so I can get over you?

I flopped onto my back and stared up at the ceiling. "I bet that would go over well."

Mai's words came back to haunt me.

If anything personal arises, you'll be done at the company...

Well.

THE VIRGIN

Sex got pretty downright personal, right?
But if that was my end goal, I needed to move things along.
Rolling out of my bed, I eyed the suits in my closet.
Just how in the hell do you go about seducing somebody?

Chapter Five

WEEK ONE *Mission Seduce The Boss* complete. Not that I was actually thinking of it as an actual plan. Just...an overall goal, one I was taking this in stages.

I had to be subtle, because if I just up and planted my ass in his lap, he'd figured it out. I'd be out of a job and gone before I had a chance to accomplish the goal.

But I'd gotten through the first week.

And all I'd done was make myself relax. Or at least *pretend* to relax around him.

It was too easy to do, and too often, I'd found myself *really* lowering my guard, something I could never do. Being near him, without the walls I'd built around myself made me remember the girl I'd been, the man I'd thought he was. I used to laugh with him. It was too easy to glide closer to that line. It was a line I couldn't cross and I had to remember that.

He made it hard, too, because sometimes I'd see him watching me, an odd look in his eyes that made me wonder.

But if he recognized me, if he remembered me, wouldn't he say something? Or, hey, *fire* me?

Surely he'd realized I wouldn't be working for him out of coincidence, that I didn't remember *him*, right?

So he must not remember.

Maybe he has just bought so many little hotels, made so many *acquisitions* that he can't remember them all.

And that's entirely possible. I've gone through the records. Gallagher Enterprises has more than doubled in size in the past decade, ever since the Boy Genius came along. That was what his brothers teasingly called him. All of them were architects, but he had a little something extra. That was what the articles said, at least. He knew when to buy, where to buy. When to build. A few of the acquisitions he'd made had been...questionable...some might say. Bad bets, risky.

They turned out to be the biggest and best moneymakers the company had. Had my parents' place turned out like that? I wouldn't know. I imagined I wouldn't even recognize it, but I refused to let myself so much as look it up online.

It hurt to think of it. The place I loved so much had been a risk, a bad bet. Because it *did* hurt to think of it, I pushed it out of my mind and focused on the current project.

He'd ended up bypassing the company in Dallas. Now they were looking at another company in Austin—a younger company, edgier, had a bolder outlook on things from what I could tell. "They'll want to do something more along the lines of merger, not an acquisition," he'd told me when he had me start doing the research. "He wants us to keep his people on, including him."

"And you'll do what, then?"

"If I feel it's a good move for us, then that's what we'll do. He's got a good head for business, but he took it over from his father, and the father...well. That's a different story. I'll just have to see what feels right when we sit down to meet." He'd shrugged and had me order up lunch.

Now as it ticked closer to seven, my arches were screaming and I swept notes, pens, and my tablet into my bag. "What time tomorrow, Mr. Gallagher?"

"Drake," he said again.

I sighed, putting a lot of patience into the sound. "You're not going to stop, are you?"

"I will when you start calling me Drake."

"Fine. Drake. What time tomorrow?"

He paused, leaning back in his chair. "Wow. You gave in already?"

I pretended to be confused. "You don't want me to call you Drake?"

"If I didn't, I wouldn't have asked about fifty times this week."

"I think it was sixty-two." Hitching my bag onto my shoulder, I rested a hand on my desk. "Tomorrow?"

He watched me. "Take the morning off. But I need you tomorrow night."

"Tomorrow night?"

"Charity dinner. Black tie. If you can't find anything, let Sierra know and she'll help you."

I stared at him. "Is this a business function?"

"Yes. I make business connections and I prefer not to have a dozen women trying to snare me for the next bachelor function or whatever else they might want." A faint smile slanted his lips and his eyes were unreadable. The sun's dying light filtered through the tinted glass and he angled his head, studying me. "Mai was comfortable attending such functions. If you're not..."

Jackass. Daring me. "It's not an issue." I turned on my heel. Great. Another night in heels. Had to find a dress. Had to spend the night looking at him in a fucking tux.

I refused to admit my palms were a little sweaty just thinking of it.

———— ◉ ————

IN RETROSPECT, I UNDERSTOOD why he wanted somebody with him.

He kept me on his arm almost the entire night. He didn't drink alcohol, he spoke with a number of people and I lost track of the cards he had pushed into his palm. Many of which were pushed into mine, a few were carelessly discarded.

Several times, he leaned over and murmured into my ear, "I want you to give him a call next week." Or "When he calls, I'm not in. Ever."

Sometimes, he had a sly little comment to add which strained my patience because I wasn't supposed to be snickering as somebody walked away.

Then came a tall, slim brunette. She could have passed for my older, much more polished sister. If I had one, and if she was loaded. The diamonds at her neck were discreet and tasteful, the silk dress she wore was the sort of designer piece that I only wished I'd allow myself to indulge in. But where would I wear such a thing? Other than...well...an event like this. I did have money, thanks to my parents, but it wouldn't last if I made such foolish indulges but my, what a lovely indulgence. It fell over her curves like jeweled mist and part of me sighed with envy.

She cast me a dismissive glance. "This is your latest guard dog, Drake?"

His hand settled more firmly at the small of my back. "My admin, Shannon. Shannon, this is Myra Fairbanks. Her husband heads up the charity."

She didn't even look at me. "And where is Mai?"

"She's left me, I'm afraid. I'm heartbroken, but Shannon is helping me through."

Myra took a step closer, lifted a hand.

Before she could make contact, Drake backed up. It was subtle, careful. But very clear. *Don't touch...*

"Aw, lover," she purred. "I just wanted to ask if you had time to slip away for a moment."

"Would your husband mind?" I asked.

Her eyes flashed to me. "I wasn't speaking to you."

I blinked at her. "If you need to make an appointment with Mr. Gallagher, I'll take your information and see if he has anything open on his schedule. But I hardly see that this is the place for personal assignations, especially as your husband is looking this way." I glanced past her, nodding at the man with distinguished silver hair and a black mustache. I'd met him earlier. He'd seemed kind, with a big, boisterous laugh and when he spoke of the children the charity would help, you could see his heart in his eyes.

Her eyes, pale blue and glittering, remained on me for a long moment. Then she turned on her heel and swayed away.

"An assignation," he mused.

"I'm not carrying a thesaurus," I said. "If you're unfamiliar with the meaning, you'll have to look it up later."

He chuckled. "You handle her about as well as Mai does. She won't like you for it."

"She likes you even less." Myra was glaring at us from behind the rim of a martini glass.

"She hasn't liked me for quite a while." He gave me a sidelong look. "Ever since I refused to repeat an assignation."

"Well. Perhaps you shouldn't have indulged the first time. She looks like she's high maintenance." The words slipped out of me before I could stop them and I looked away as his laugh echoed through the room.

"Indeed. Come on. We've got more palms to shake. I want to get out of here sometime before midnight."

<hr />

IT WAS ELEVEN-FORTY-nine when the car pulled away from the hotel.

I resisted the urge to slip off my shoes, but I couldn't stop myself from rolling my ankles and curling my toes against the padded bed. A moment later, a warm hand closed around my ankle. I tensed, shooting a look at him.

He wasn't looking at me.

He was almost determinedly *not* looking at me as he lifted my foot up.

This...

My breath caught as he loosened the strap. "I don't see how you women wear these," he murmured as he set the ball of his thumb against my instep.

"Mr. Gallagher."

His gaze lifted and he stared at me through his lashes. "Drake. It's Drake. Remember...?" His voice was soft, but unyielding all the same.

Yet I wasn't thinking about that firm suggestion.

*Remember...*I swallowed against the knot in my throat as memory practically assailed me. There had been a time...

Stop. Don't think about that.

"This is very much unnecessary," I said, tugging my foot.

He applied firm pressure to the arch and a groan erupted out of me. "Sounds like it is necessary."

"My feet hurt," I said sourly. "That doesn't mean *you* need to rub them."

"So you don't want me touching you?" he asked, his voice soft.

"I..."

The denial locked in my throat.

"That's hardly the point," I said, forcing the words out. "It's not appropriate."

A grin, dark and wicked, slashed across his lips. "It's a foot rub. Inappropriate would be..." His voice trailed off and he looked away. "Perhaps we shouldn't discuss that. But if you want me to stop...?"

He paused.

I continued to stare at him, my heart racing, my breathing ragged.

Just a foot rub.

Slowly, I relaxed. "Just a foot rub."

He resumed that wonderful touch and I could have whimpered, could have moaned. I almost melted into a puddle on the seat. As he shifted his attention to my other foot, it dawned on me that I was practically sprawled on the seat now, my feet in his lap, my head against the side of the car, my weight half propped on my elbow.

"I'm disappointed, Shannon," he said, a sad sigh escaping him. Something cold trickled down my back.

"What?"

I went to pull my feet away. Was this some sort of test? The jerk—

He tightened his hold on my ankle, shrugging as he watched me out of the corner of his eye. "I was sort of hoping you'd ask what the inappropriate things are. I left it wide open there. I thought perhaps you'd ask what I was referring to."

Nerves skittered. Bloomed. Staring at him, I tugged on my feet, insistent this time and he let go. Curling up in the corner of the seat, watching him, I shook my head. "A foot rub is harmless enough, right? No reason to worry about anything else. You're my boss and—"

In my mind, I saw how I'd like for this to play out. He would shift to his knees on the floor in front of me. Then he would kiss me. Maybe he'd say something. *Tell me I shouldn't.*

But if he tried, I doubted I would say anything at all. Because it was something I'd wanted for ten years.

He didn't move. The car glided to a smooth stop and his gaze shifted past my shoulder to the window. "It looks like we're here. I'll walk you up."

<hr/>

HIS HAND RESTED AT the base of my spine. Through the thin silk of my dress, I was almost excruciatingly aware of that touch, the warmth of his hand, how his thumb stroked, almost absently over my spine as we mounted the steps.

In my right hand, I gripped my keys. In my left, I carried my shoes, those pretty, sparkly, strappy heels that had looked wonderful on me but felt like sheer torture as the evening went on. Under the soles of my feet, the paved stones of the walk were smooth and cool. Overhead, the brilliant lights of the city lit the sky.

And next to me, Gallagher walked and waited, a patient, quiet presence.

Waiting for something. I didn't know what. But there was something. I could feel it, like one of my pretty, sparkling shoes had yet to drop.

I wanted to turn around and yell at him, tell him to say what he had to say and then get his ass back in the car.

I turned to tell him to do just that, and then I noticed.

The car was no longer waiting at the curb.

My gut tightened and I clutched my keys tighter while my heart knocked against my ribs.

"Where is Jake?"

"I told him to drive around the block. I'll give him a call shortly." He reached for the keys I held clutched too tightly in my fist and took them from me, fitting one expertly to the lock, without even needing to search for the right one. For some reason, that just irritated me more.

As he unlocked the deadbolt, I wrapped my arms around myself and managed not to shiver. The night had turned cool, but there wasn't enough bite in the air to justify needing a wrap. I hated to carry one and I always forgot them anyway. He turned to me, the dim light painting that deep red hair of his nearly black. "After you," he said, his voice low.

"You don't need to see me in."

He cocked a brow. "Perhaps there is something I need to discuss with you."

Barely, I managed to keep from curling my lip at him. Just barely. I slid inside and disarmed the alarm as he shut the door behind me. My heart hammered in my chest, that silly, foolish little fantasy settling in my mind again. Him kneeling before me, his mouth on mine.

Another kiss.

His body pressed to mine.

Him fulfilling that promise he'd made all those years ago.

Hurtful words undone. Could that happen? Could we go back to who we had been on the beach, him a too-solemn, serious young man and me a foolish, hopeful girl who hadn't had her heart, her dreams, her world smashed, all within the span of a couple of months?

Perhaps if I reached for him, took what I'd wanted then, if he'd let me, I could find some small piece of that girl I'd been. And some *peace*. I'd never forget the misery of the months that followed, the loneliness of the years that came later. The loss would still be there, as would the shattered dreams, the awful nightmares, mornings when I woke to the sound of my own choked screams. But if I could find...closure...yes. That was what I needed. Was this why I was here?

Was *that* why I had come here, seeking him?

What would closure give me, I wondered. The loss will be there. The pain will not fade. And everything he took from you will still be his.

No. I didn't need closure. I needed to end this, because this would solve nothing.

Taking a deep, bracing breath, I turned.

And the breath stuttered out of me as I found him just scant inches away, his face lost in the shadows. "Mr. Gallagher," I said, his name catching on my lips.

"Drake." He reached up, flicked a lock of hair behind my ear.

My heart skittered inside my chest and the ache within me spread.

"Drake. I—"

"You didn't ask what the inappropriate things are," he murmured, moving even closer, until even the *thought* of personal space died. I could feel the heat of him, so close, warming my skin. Under the silk of my dress and the strapless bra I wore, my breasts ached, feeling too full, while my nipples went tight. My thighs felt like putty. Leaning back against the table, I braced my weight on my hands and tried to pierce the darkness to better see his face.

"I beg your pardon?"

"You never asked," he said, his heat crowding in around me, his scent flooding my head and it was like I was lost. Again. Lost in the time, years ago, when life was simple and easy and sweet. When things made sense and there was no pain. Just me, just him, and the promise of the life I'd thought would be mine.

He reached up and cupped my cheek, so close that all I could see was the gleam of his eyes. "Is this inappropriate, Shan?" he murmured, his mouth just a whisper away, our breaths mingling.

A warning alarm sounded in my head.

"I—"

"What about this?" He curved one hand over my waist, tugged me closer. "I'm almost positive this is. But you know what?"

He pressed his mouth to mine. "I don't give a flying fuck."

And just then, neither did I.

I opened for him, shuddering as his tongue stroked across my lips and then, with calm assurance, he took my mouth and I swayed against him. Curling my fingers into his jacket, I realized I had no idea what it was like to be lost. *This*, here, *this* was lost. Lost in the heat of his kiss, the heat of his body and the pleasure of his touch as he slid his hand up my back and tangled it in my hair.

He wrapped his free arm around me and boosted me onto the table at my back. It was hip-height, long and narrow and as he settled me on it, I realized I paid far too little attention to it when I purchased it. Was it sturdy enough for this? Just then, I didn't care. As long as I could stay right here, nothing else mattered.

His mouth left mine, his tongue flicking at the corner of my mouth, his lips brushing along my cheek before he caught my earlobe between his teeth. "Still so sweet, Shan. You still taste so fucking good," he whispered, his voice a low, rough croon in my ear as he angled my head back, tugging on my hair until he had me where he wanted me. Then his tongue was tracing along my lips once more, pushing into my mouth and I couldn't stop shuddering, couldn't stop shaking. I caught his tongue between my teeth and bit down, just a bit, and felt like flying when he growled against me, yanked me closer and started to rock, the solid length of his cock a brand between my legs.

Through my panties, I could feel him. And I felt myself as well, wet and slick and so ready for him.

Now. That was all I could think. Finally, now.

"Shan..."

That warning, again. Turning into a scream.

His hand tangled in my hair, tugged my head back and he moved to my throat, his teeth scraping along, sending delightful little shivers through me. He'd done that before. I'd always loved it. He'd do that, whisper my name...

My name.

Son of a bitch.

Sucking in a breath, I gathered up strength and shoved him away.

"You bastard."

He stumbled backward, his hair falling into his eyes as he stared at me.

"What?"

"Odd time to decide you remember me."

A weird little grin crooked his lips. "Who said I just now remembered?" He moved back and when I would have tried to slip off the table to get away, he bracketed me in place with his arms. My body shuddered, trembled at his nearness. His lips brushed my ear as he murmured, "The second I saw your name on the list of candidates, I knew who you were. The only questions *I* had was why you were trying to get a job in my company, and whether you knew who you were going to be working for. If you got the job. But you knew. That's why you applied. I saw it the minute you looked at me."

I tensed, fought the urge to look away as he lifted up, his piercing gaze cutting right through me. I said nothing. He was right, of course. But nothing could make me *admit* that.

"Why?" he asked, catching a lock of my hair and wrapping it around his finger. "Tell me, Shan. Why did you want this job? What do you want from me?"

Tell him.

I fought the urge to sneer at him, fought the urge to blush. Fought the urge to turn away so he wouldn't see the blush creeping up my neck to stain my cheeks a horrible, awful red. I could feel it, that burning blush that made my skin feel two sizes too small.

Worse, I could still feel the need inside me. That burning, aching need and I knew if my brain hadn't clicked on, if I hadn't started to *think*, I would probably still be wrapped around him, clutching at him.

And I'd know. I'd have the answer, I'd know what I'd missed all these years. I kind of hated my brain in that moment.

What would he do, I wondered, if I reached down, cupped him through his trousers, stroked him. Told him that I wanted what he'd made me want ten years ago. What I'd dreamed about ever since. What he'd do if I told him that I couldn't have another man because everyone I looked at came up short. The kind ones might fill the void left by loneliness but none of them filled the emptiness inside me.

Silent, I stared at him.

Slowly, he backed away. He must have seen something on my face, something that warned him, or clued in him that too much of me had changed. An assessing look entered his eyes and he tucked his hands into his pockets as he continued to study me, like he was taking me in, piecing together all changes, subtle and otherwise, that he might have overlooked.

But the biggest changes lie within, and I wouldn't let him see those.

"Just why are you here?" he asked, his voice soft, wondering.

For some reason, it sent a chill running through me. I don't understand why. But I didn't let my discomfort show as I shrugged. "I need a job. Isn't that why most people work?"

"This wasn't what you wanted to do with your life, Shan." He shook his head, never taking his eyes from me.

"Shannon," I bit off. Shan no longer existed. We'd buried her, the day we buried my father. Before that, most likely.

"Plans change." I gave him an easy shrug as I scooted off the table and struggled to adjust my dress. "Mine changed drastically that summer and this is the road my life put me on. Besides, you have to admit, I'm good at what I do."

"Yes. You are. Almost too good." He continued to study me. He started to pace around me in a circle. I turned with him, refusing to let him out of my sight. "You're angry. I knew you were—I'd seen it before, even though you kept it hidden. You're not bothering now. It was business, Shan. I..." He stopped, stared out the window. "I could be a total ass and say it was never anything more than business, but that changed after the first two or three times you talked me into spending time with you."

He rubbed his neck, his expression shuttered. "You never did have to try hard." He slid me a look. "I convinced myself that it was harmless, you know. I knew it wasn't but up until that last night on the beach, I managed to fool myself. I can understand if you're pissed off at me. I was a bastard, and never should have allowed things to get personal between us when I was doing business with your parents."

I felt cold, uneasy, while a slippery ugly weight settled in my gut. "You can understand," I said, echoing his words. There was an ache inside me. A hollow, empty one, spreading throughout me, so wide, so all-encompassing, I thought it just might drive *me* out and I'd cease to exist. I'd just be...emptiness.

"I was wrong."

Flicking him a look, I turned away and moved into the kitchen. There was a wine cooler built into the island and if I thought my hands would be steady, I would have opened myself a bottle, had a glass. I needed it. But my fingers were trembling. Curling them over the edge of the counter, I gripped it and tried to breathe around the huge, hollow ache. "Is that all you've got to say?"

"What else do you want me to say? I shouldn't have let things get personal between us when I was doing business. It was a mistake, and one I've never repeated since then."

His footsteps were muffled on the carpet and then I heard the soft whisper as they hit the tile flooring of the kitchen. I shivered, tried to convince my legs to move, but I felt frozen there. Frozen and trapped as he reached up and brushed his fingers down my neck. "That is, until now. I never let myself get involved with anybody I had a business connection to. Not even remotely. And then there you were, and it's like it's ten years ago. How do you pull me in like this?"

His lips brushed my neck.

Heat exploded through me and that snapped the spell.

Jerking away from him, I slid around the island and turned to glare at him.

"Don't." The word came out of my throat like I had to drag it over glass, broken and jagged. Glaring at him, while my knees went weak and everything inside me melted, I shook my head. "You don't get to stand there and say you were *wrong*, that was just business, brush it all off just like that and then put your hands on me."

"You want my hands on you."

He circled around the island.

I started to back away, but then, feeling like a silly little child, I planted my feet and glared at him, angling my chin up.

He caught it in his hand, tipping my head back and staring down into my eyes. "Even though you're furious with me—and *why* are you furious, damn it? Even though you're furious, you still want my hands on you." He dipped his head, pressed his face to my neck and breathed me in.

I shuddered. My knees threatened to give out, and my strength all but abandoned me. Swaying, I slammed one hand against the island

and although I knew I shouldn't, I clutched at him with the other hand. "Drake…"

"That's it," he whispered, his lips stroking across my skin. "Say my name."

A fog of lust clouded my head.

One of his hands curved over my hip, stroked, his fingers spread wide. As he slid it around to the small of my back, his mouth closed over mine.

Should I do this?

He pulled me against him, hard, and I felt the long, heavy length of his cock against me.

Oh, yes.

It was a slow, maybe even unnoticeable surrender. I'd stood against him, not rigidly, but not exactly welcoming. Now, I let my hands wander, down his chest to tug his shirt from the waistband of his pants, under that crisp white cloth to seek out the warmth of skin, the hardness of muscle.

Those muscles jumped as I ran my fingers along his sides. Ticklish. He was ticklish. If I could have thought, that discovery might have delighted me.

As it was, I was too busy trying to breathe as he spun me around and put me on the island. It was cool beneath me, and hard.

One hand pushed my skirt up.

The other sought out the hidden zipper at my side.

"You drive me insane." He said those words calmly, like he was dictating a note, but as he lifted his head to look down at me, the look in his eyes was anything but calm, anything but cool. And I all but moaned as he reached up and ran his hand straight down the midline of my torso, stopping only where the material of my dress bunched at my middle.

He caught the material and tugged it down, leaving me clad in nothing but the strapless bra and panties.

Beneath my back, the marble was a cool relief against my overheated skin. Then his hands closed around my waist and I wasn't thinking about the marble, or how I'd suddenly become so much hotter.

His mouth pressed to my hipbone. Reaching up, I gasped, my fingers curling into his short hair, tangling in those dark red strands. He kissed a line across my lower belly, just above the lace of my panties.

When he lifted his head, his eyes cut into me, stark, hungry, so intense. It was a look that made me shudder, made me want.

He lifted, slowly, bracing his hands beside my shoulders as he peered down into my face. Our gazes held for a long moment, the silence taut between us. Neither of us spoke, but a thousand words seemed to pass between us.

If only I could understand those unspoken words on *his* part.

His hand pushed into my hair and I followed his subtle urging, sitting up. Once I was upright, he slid a hand down my back and I felt the catch on my bra give away. Then it was gone and nothing separated me from him but the thin silk of my panties.

It wasn't enough.

I wanted to pull back. Wanted to hide.

After all this time, I was suddenly terrified.

His hands cupped my face and he pressed a soft, gentle kiss to each eye, my cheeks, taking his time before he worked his way down to my mouth. As his tongue stroked across my lips, I reached up, clutching at his wrists. Deep inside me, something started to pulse—that hunger. A deep, unshakable sort of need. It had slumbered inside me all of this time and now that he was here, now that this was happening, again, it was like a beast, threatening to take me over.

Arching against him, I pressed myself to him, felt that power of him through that sleek, sexy suit.

THE VIRGIN

He growled against my lips and tugged my hair, pulling me back from him. "Stop," he muttered, pressing his brow to mine. "Or this might just be over before it begins."

"I don't want to stop." Staring into his eyes, hoping he didn't sense the desperation in me, I let go of his wrist and reached down, cupping him through his trousers. I stroked, up, then down. This, here, was one thing I could do. Perhaps I'd never actually had sex with a man, but that didn't mean I was completely inexperienced.

His lids drooped as I stroked my thumb across the blunt, rounded head and when I dragged my hand back down and cupped the sac of his balls, he snarled and yanked me against him, capturing my hands and pinning them behind me as he started to pump against me. Fast, short little strokes that had the wet silk of my panties dragging over my clitoris in a teasing caress. I cried out against his mouth while that pulsing deep inside me tightened, drawing me tight. I felt it, a queer little heat spreading through me.

And then he sank his teeth into my lower lip. The heat inside spread, grew larger. My skin felt tight, too tight and I couldn't breathe. There just wasn't enough air, but my heart was racing, hammering—

"Come for me," he muttered against my mouth.

I can't—

But I was. With a sob, I climaxed against him, just like that, so easily as he rocked me back and forth against the ridge of his shaft.

I sobbed out his name and he all but breathed out mine, almost a blessing, his voice reverent and hushed.

"Shan..."

Panting, I lifted my gaze to his, staring at him, trying not to let him see how deeply this affected me.

His eyes were turbulent, full of emotions I couldn't even describe.

A moment later, he hooked his fingers in the straps of silk that ran over my hips. I felt a jerk, a twist, then the silk fell uselessly away. "Not waiting another minute." He pushed my thighs apart. "We've waited too long."

Yes. Yes, we had. I clutched at his shoulders as he reached down, freeing himself from his trousers.

I didn't dare look down.

I'd managed not to let him realize—*yet*.

Because the nerves were tangling, twisting inside me, because that voice had risen up to jeer at me in the back of my mind...*I don't fuck naïve little virgins*...I leaned forward and pressed my mouth to his chest. The starched fabric of his tuxedo shirt separated us and I fisted my hands in it, hating the barrier.

His hand cupped the back of my neck, twisting in my hair. "Look at me," he rasped. His voice, low and guttural, stroked over me like a velvet glove.

Shivering, I tipped my head, letting my lashes fall to shield my eyes.

Between my legs, I felt the press of his cock. Naked, thick, hard. My mouth fell open and his gaze dropped, lingering on my lips.

I whimpered as he wrapped a hand around his length and teased me, using the head to stroke over me, once, twice, three times, before he parted me, taking the caress deeper. My mouth fell open on a hungry moan while his vicious snarl bounced off this walls. "So fucking wet...that's it, baby. Let me feel..."

Abruptly, he swore, tensing as he slowly pulled back. My body screamed in denial as he slammed a fist against the counter. "Fuck. I...no condoms," he muttered, his eyes going dark, narrowing to slits.

No. I...I can't lose this now...

Reaching down, I trailed the tip of my finger over the crown of him. He was wet. Slowly, I looked down, stared at the ruddy, swollen head. A bead of fluid gathered on the crest and unwittingly, I licked my lips. Oh. Oh...my.

His hand tangled in my hair, yanking my head back. "Fuck. Stop it, Shan. Didn't you hear me? I don't have anything with me."

"I don't need it," I said, the words spilling out of me. "I'm on the pill."

"You need it for more than that." His features were hooded.

I never had. But I didn't think this was the ideal time to point it out to him. I had to take the pill for other reasons, so pregnancy wasn't much of a concern. I'd never needed protection for anything else. But this wasn't really the time to mention that because I wasn't going to risk him pulling back...again.

I arched, pressing one knee to his hip. "I've been...busy...for a while. No time. I've always been careful." That wasn't a lie. How much more careful could a *virgin* get?

"I'm..." He groaned as I wiggled against him. "That's not..."

I slid my hand between us and his gaze locked on it. I'd intended to touch *him*, but instinct had me doing something else. Smiling a little, I trailed my fingers up my thigh. "If you're not interested, Gallagher, just say so. I'll handle it myself then. I'm used to it."

A dare.

Harsh flags of color rose on his cheeks and he caught my wrists once more. Pinning them at my back, he muttered, "You fucking little brat."

Victory was a sweet, sweet thrill in my chest as he angled his head, took my mouth again.

And then, he took me.

I felt him nudging at my entrance, slow at first, my body resisting him. A dark, hungry little growl escaped him as he lifted his mouth, his eyes cutting to me as he let go of my wrists to shift his grip to my hips. "Fuck...you're so tight. Relax, baby...relax..."

The sound of his voice was a velvet caress against my senses, one hand steady at my hips as he withdrew and then surged against me. Slow, steady...again, and again, each shallow thrust taking him a little deeper.

But still, I resisted him. I gasped at his invasion, feeling too tight and full of him already.

Pain flared and without realizing it, I tensed, tried to pull away.

"No," he muttered, gripping my hip. "Just..."

He surged deep and I cried out as he buried his cock completely inside, pain splitting through me.

A ragged, high cry escaped me and it was done.

His eyes, startled, sought mine out.

"Shan..."

Beneath the pain, something glorious and thrilling rode me. Curling my arms around him, tighter, I whispered his name.

He pulled back, surged in deeper. That slice of pain lingered, but this time, sweet, beautiful ecstasy rolled through me and I moaned, shuddering around him. The head of his cock stroked me, just *there* as he fucked it into me and it was bliss. Pure, sheer bliss. Each thrust, each stroke of his body left me dazed.

And all the while, he stared at me.

If I could have thought, if I could have focused, I would have seen it.

The knowledge in his eyes.

But it wouldn't have mattered.

I had this...I had *him*.

For now.

Pain mingled with the pleasure as he rolled his hips against mine. He hunkered down over me, his body forcing mine flat back onto the island until both of us where on top of it. I felt us sliding across it and I drove my heels down, bracing myself for those glorious, deep thrusts. One arm came up, hooking under my shoulders to help steady me. The other cupped my hip, his thumb stroking over my skin, a soft, delicate little caress that shouldn't have had much of an impact, but I felt it, deep in my core.

THE VIRGIN

His teeth raked down my neck and then he caught my earlobe, bit me lightly.

I cried out his name and felt him swell inside me. "Shan."

That was all he said. I said something else, felt it tear out of me. His name, maybe something else. I was desperate for him, so desperate. Just as I'd always been.

And then I exploded. It was like I exploded into him and ceased to exist.

If only that was how it really played out, life would have been so much easier.

Chapter Six

THE BED WAS SOFT UNDER me.

The air was cool around me.

And his arm was a heavy weight around my waist, all but pinning me in place.

I'd slept.

Dreamlessly, I slept. No nightmares, and no haunting dreams of the two of us on the beach, either. Just...peace. As my lids came open, I was brutally aware of his silence and the soreness of my body.

Could I slip out of the bed? Go shower, I thought. Compose myself and figure out how to go on from here—

His hand spread wide over my belly and his lips touched my shoulder. "You're awake."

Closing my eyes, I scratched that plan. I'd just have to fake the composure.

That was okay. I'd been faking my way through life for a very, very long time.

"It would appear you are, too," I said, keeping my voice level as I stared out the round window situated in the middle of the wall. During the day, it faced out over the garden. That was another plus my apartment had. The building had four tenants and the owner kept the top floor to himself. He also had full control of the backyard, although we were allowed to *enjoy* it, as he'd phrased it. Just then, I wouldn't mind being out in the backyard, with a stiff drink, while I figured a way out of the mess I'd created.

The mess...

I closed my eyes, turning my face into my pillow.

A hand stroked down my hair and Drake kissed my neck.

"We need to talk."

"I'm not much for pillow talk," I grumbled, my cheeks going red as I imagined just what he might want to talk about. Maybe he would be up for distractions. Rolling around, I reached down and found that he was naked. Just as I'd hoped. Naked, and already hard, although he hardened even more against my palm. "If I'm in bed, I'd rather be doing other things. This sounds more fun."

Truth be told, I'd wondered about this...a lot. What would it be like, to lie next to him, feel the warmth of him next to me, speak to him in soft, quiet voices while our skin cooled and our hearts slowed.

It would have been rather wonderful.

Except the talk he wanted to have wasn't anything I wanted to share in.

Under my hand, his cock was hard, silk stretched over iron and when I stroked him, he pulsed in my hand. I felt an answering pulse deep in my pussy. Why talk, anyway? Sex sounded better.

His lids drooped and he moved into my hand, then, to my shock, he rolled me onto my back, caught my hands and pinned them over my head. "We talk," he said, his voice flat, his cock a brand against my belly. My pussy throbbed, ached. He was so close...so close. "Then, we can do whatever you want in bed."

"Whatever..." I heaved out a sigh and focused on the shadowy ceiling. "Why can't we do that first?"

"Because you seem determined *not* to talk."

Jerking one shoulder in a shrug, I flicked a look at him. His face could have been carved out of stone. "I don't see any reason *to* talk, baby." Then, because hiding behind a mask was safer, I let a smile play over my lips. "Really, Drake. I'd think you'd be happy. Ten years ago, all I *ever* wanted to do was talk your ear off and try to get you to stop being so serious. To have fun. I didn't understand how serious work was—how serious *life* was. I was just a silly, foolish girl who had no reason wasting your time, but I've learned my lesson. Talking is waste of time. Why bother with it?"

"You..." he stopped. Shook his head.

He pulled away from me and I felt cold, lying there without his body to warm me.

"You weren't foolish, and you weren't silly." His voice was clipped and short.

He'd turned his back to me and I sat there, pulling the blanket around me. It did nothing to warm me, though. His spine was a long, rigid line, his shoulders just as tense. "I was the foolish one, Shan. I was seven years older, and I never should have gotten involved with you. But I did and..."

He stopped, sighed.

"No point dwelling on the past," I said, forcing the words out in a light tone even though it all but choked me.

No point...

I was such a hypocrite. Such a fool.

I did *nothing* but dwell on the past. Nothing but let it drag me down, all but strangling me with its chains.

I went to climb from the bed, my legs rubbery but as I started to rise, his hands caught my shoulders, tugging me back against him.

"Why?"

I stared at the window, the way the moonlight glinted off the glass. "Why what?" I asked numbly.

"Why did you lie to me?"

There was no point in lying to him. "I didn't lie. I'm pretty sure *never* counts as a long time, Drake. And you don't get much more careful than *virgin*."

His sigh kissed my cheek and then he slid his arm around my waist, tugged me back against him. "Let's try this...why didn't you *tell* me?"

When I opened my mouth, I didn't know what I expected to come out. It certainly wasn't the laugh. That long, bitter laugh that didn't stop until I was all but doubled over, aching from it, ready to cry.

His hand stroked up and down my back. "Shan...talk to me."

I batted his hand away and climbed out of the bed. This time, he made no move to stop me.

"Why didn't I tell you?" I parroted back to him as I opened the closet and pulled out the robe I'd left on the hook there. The soft silk did nothing to warm me, but I needed some sort of barrier before I faced him.

Over the expanse of the darkened bedroom, I glared at him.

"Ten years ago, you rather plainly told me... *I don't fuck naïve little virgins*," I said, mimicking that tone. Oh, I knew it well. I'd heard those words. So many times, in my sleep. They'd left some of the deepest scars on me, but it wasn't just the *words*. It was how he had looked at me as he said it. That scathing, dismissive look.

"I didn't want to burden you with my virginity," I said, jerking my hair free from the collar of my robe until it could hang down the back. As he climbed off the bed, staring at me, his expression stark, I angled up my chin and glared at him. "It was my...*problem* and I chose how to handle it. You don't need to concern yourself with it. You just happened to own the dick that ended it."

Turning on my heel, I stormed into the bathroom just behind me.

I snapped the lock into place as I heard him striding toward me.

"Open the door, Shannon."

"There's no need," I said sourly. "You wanted to talk. Fine. We talked. Now I want you to leave."

Pressing my head against the door, I sucked in a deep breath, desperate for air.

And I listened.

It was a very, very long time before I heard the sound of his footsteps.

THE VIRGIN

———————⊙———————

SUNDAY IT RAINED.

All day.

A cold, dreary rain that kept me penned up in the house. Some part of me wistfully thought of the pretty little apartment a block away, with a window seat and a rooftop garden. I could have spent the day curled in that window seat with a blanket, a book, and booze. Booze might ease the misery inside me, at least for a while.

I was giving it the old college try, anyway.

The better part of a bottle of wine hadn't done anything to erase the misery, though, and I sat on the couch, staring out the floor to ceiling windows of my sterile little condo, shivering despite the blanket and trying to figure out the next step.

I'd accomplished what I set out to do.

I'd just wanted to be with him.

Only once.

A book lay next to me, untouched.

Reaching for the mostly empty glass of wine, I cradled it against my chest and let my mind wander.

What next.

Did I truly want to go back to working for him, knowing that he knew, that he'd known all along?

Did I want to see whatever emotion he might feel for me?

Then, as I sat there, confused and tired, Mai's words came back to haunt me.

If anything personal arises, you'll be done at the company.

I'll be done.

Swallowing, I shifted my gaze to the laptop computer lying on the coffee table.

So far, he hadn't called, not even once.

That was, well, unusual.

Normally he would have called several times to go over the schedule for the coming week, to make sure I was ready for the trip we had coming up on Thursday. But he hadn't called. Not even once.

With a hand that shook, I reached for the computer.

No. I didn't like this job, but he'd thrown me out on my ass before. Not literally, perhaps, but the result had been the same. Everything that came after was the result of that. I couldn't go through that again.

The knot inside my chest spread and my hands started to shake. "Maybe I should have thought this through better."

With the laptop in hand, I shifted around and put the wine down on the table next to me.

I was done here.

I'd done what I set out to do.

He'd gone through a number of admins in a short period of time before. Would it really surprise anybody if I left so soon?

It settled wrong, doing it this way. It felt like I was giving up.

But I'd rather quit than be forced out.

My terms. I'd do it on my terms.

<hr />

I WORE RED ON MONDAY.

Red was a power color.

It brought me confidence and confidence was something I desperately needed as the car came to a stop in front of my condo. Jake came around to open the door for me and he paused a bit before he opened the door. "Is everything okay, Ms. Crosby?"

"Of course, Jake. Why wouldn't it be?" I had a resignation letter tucked inside my bag and there was a lump in my chest as I slid into the car.

The empty car. I frowned and looked over at him. "Where is Mr. Gallagher?"

"We're picking him up on the way. He needed a few more minutes."

I nodded and settled back in the seat as he shut the door.

He needed a few more minutes. Frowning, I tucked my hands in my lap and looked outside. I wouldn't think about it. It wasn't anything I needed to concern myself with, really.

Jake moved smoothly into the traffic. The question leaped from me without me realizing it had even formed in my mind. "Do you know what the hold-up was?"

Jake seemed to know *everything*, something I'd already figured out in the few short weeks I'd been around. He slid me a look in the mirror, shrugged. "He was meeting with Hannah and Ms. Gibbens, I think." Then he blew out a sigh. "You'll probably be hearing about it, whatever it is. There was a look in his eye when I dropped him off. Heads are going to roll, and soon, if I know the man."

My palms started to sweat.

And I was painfully aware of that resignation letter. Although it waited in the bag I had tucked on the floor next to my feet, it felt like a weight, one that hung around my shoulders.

Perhaps I should have emailed and given him a heads-up.

I'd be damned if he fired me.

Chapter Seven

IF HEADS WERE GOING to roll that day, mine wasn't on the chopping block. Not yet, at least.

It was six o'clock when he looked at me and said brusquely, "We're done for the day."

Not once did I ever learn just why he'd been late that morning—and he'd been nearly two hours late. Jake had taken me to a local hospital where Gallagher Enterprises was helping to fund a children's wing and I'd had to run interference for Drake, answering questions, asking the ones Drake had noted in his file. Fortunately, I'd been the one to put the file together so I knew it inside and out.

The meeting had less than thirty minutes to go when Drake had appeared, settling into his seat without even looking at me.

I felt the dismissal like a cut.

And that had been the order of the day.

There was nothing discussed but business.

He didn't look at me, except to discuss meetings, request information...basically everything I wished my job had been from the beginning.

Now he was staring at me with intense eyes as I packed my bag. "There are no meetings scheduled tomorrow until noon, when you're meeting with your brothers," I said, keeping my voice steady, thinking of the resignation letter. I hadn't had a good time to present it. Did I just leave it on his desk?

He rose from his chair.

I tensed as he came around to stand behind me. He reached up and smoothed a hand down my shoulder, I closed my eyes. "Should I be here at seven or will eight work?"

He pressed his mouth to my neck. "Come home with me."

"That wouldn't be wise," I said softly.

His hands slid my skirt up. "Why not?"

"It just wouldn't." He slid his fingers inside the waistband of my panties and my knees buckled. "Drake—"

"You went back to calling me Mr. Gallagher all fucking day," he whispered, his lips against my ear. "Are you going to call me Mr. Gallagher when I'm fucking you?"

"You..." My mouth was terribly dry. "You can't—"

The rasping of his zipper was terribly loud. "I can. And unless you say no, I'm going to."

His hand urged me forward and I found myself bent down, face forward over the desk. "Yes or no, Shan," he said and I felt his hands on my ass, spreading me.

Turning my head, I caught sight of us in the treated glass. As dark it was, it had turned the glass to a dark mirror and I could see him, the way he looked at me, the way he watched me.

"Yes."

"Yes," he muttered, his voice guttural. Then it was a snarl as he pushed the fat, rounded head against me. He slid a hand up my spine, closed it around my neck and kept it there, holding me face down. It was the most erotic sensation—I was trapped by him, surrounded by him as he fucked me and I loved it. "So fucking wet. So fucking hot. I'm not wearing a condom. I don't want one between us—I don't want *anything* between us. Tell me you don't, either."

My knees trembled and the muscles in my pussy clenched around him. "I don't want the condom."

He was asking for more. But that was all I could give him.

The hand on the back of my neck tightened. "Tell me you want me."

Closing my eyes against the tableau playing out in front of me, I pressed my face to the cool wood of my desk. "I want you." *I'll always want you.*

And it was nothing more than the truth. But this was all I'd give myself.

He gave me one inch, then withdrew. Slowly, so very slowly. Fed me that inch again, and another, as one hand on my hip held me still and kept me from moving back on him. I wanted to ride him—the instinct to do just that rose inside me, but his hold prevented me and I twisted, uselessly, straining against him.

"Mine..." The word came from him on a groan as he withdrew again, and then surged deeper. It was a slow, thorough possession and the strength drained out of me. If it wasn't for the desk that supported me and the strength of his hands, I would have dissolved into a puddle at his feet.

Drake seated himself fully inside me and I moaned, shivering around him, feeling the muscles in my cunt tighten, clutch at him as he held there. He just held there, not moving. "Drake, please..."

"That's what I need," he said. "I want to hear my name on your lips. I need to know you feel it, too, Shan. That you want me."

He started to fuck me, then. Deep, slow, and hard, and I felt each thrust echo through me, the pleasure vicious, violent waves that battered at me. Consumed me.

That hand on my neck moved away, slammed down on the desk next to my head. The other gripped my hip, his fingers digging in. I lifted my butt to meet each thrust, working my elbows beneath me so I could lift up.

His hand tangled in my hair and he half-lifted, half-twisted me until he could fuse his mouth to mine. His tongue licked at mine and I cried out against him.

The orgasm slammed into me, hard, devastating.

It was almost as devastating as I realized the truth of his words... I *was* still his.

And it was so fucking unfair.

I was always going to be.

But he would never be mine.

———◆———

HIS PHONE RANG.

It was one of those calls that he wouldn't take around me. It was his family, I suspected.

While he slid out of the room, still adjusting his clothes, I smoothed my skirt down. My heart, bruised and aching, gave a feeble beat against my ribs.

Reaching into my bag, I pulled out the letter of resignation, stared at it. The pleasure that had burned inside me just moments ago already felt like ashes.

There was a quiet sound and I looked up, found him standing in the doorway.

"I have to leave town," he said, his voice sharp.

I blinked at him. "Leave?" I echoed.

"It's unavoidable. Micah Coltrane—he used to head the offices here—is flying in to take over while I'm gone. You'll work with him until I'm back."

"Is..." I stared at the resignation. "Is there anything I can do?"

He had already dismissed me, his attention focused on whatever information he'd received just moments ago. "No. It's family business." Then, abruptly, his eyes cleared and he looked back at me.

Casually, I turned the resignation over and placed it face down as he strode toward me. He placed one finger under my chin and tilted my head back.

"I love the way you look in red," he murmured. "It suits you."

He kissed, soft and sweet. Then he was gone, long fast strides carrying him away from me.

I looked back at the resignation.

I'd hold it for a few days, make sure everything ran smoothly as this Micah Coltrane settled into place.

But I wouldn't be here when Drake came back.

Part Two

Redemption

Chapter One

THE NIGHTMARES ARE always bad this time of year. Especially here. I'd avoid this place for the rest of my life, if I could. Really, there's only one reason to come back. One reason...and one particular time of year.

My father died just two days after his birthday.

He'd been born sixty-two years ago, in this little village north of Boston.

I was born here too, and up until the summer I turned eighteen, this had been home. Then, if you'd asked if I'd ever planned to leave, make my home somewhere else, I would have laughed.

There had been no other home. This place had been it, the only home I'd ever known, the only one I'd ever wanted to know.

Then it was just ripped out from under me.

Coming back here when there was nothing to come back to just hurt.

Huddled on the bed in the bland, nondescript hotel, staring at the digital readout on the clock, I tried to force myself to stay awake. My eyelids were heavy and my eyes were gritty. Little wonder. I hadn't slept last night, but I couldn't avoid it anymore.

Not that I wouldn't try. I'd fight it as long as I could, but something told me I was about to lose that battle. It was past two in the morning. I wouldn't last much longer.

I'd read until the words blurred before my eyes. I'd already sucked down so much coffee my belly felt raw.

I couldn't stay awake. I couldn't run from the nightmares anymore.

STARING INTO THE BLANK, mechanical eye of the camera, I signed it out.

Circling my hand in front of my chest. Please. My fist on my palm—I darted a look out of the corner of my eye but he was staring everywhere, staring at everybody around us. Looking for any sign of the police.

Not at me. I finished the word. Help. Please. Help.

I'd been begging for help for three days. My grasp of sign was limited. My grandmother had been deaf and I used to be able to sign fluently, but she'd died eight years ago. Use it or lose it, right? That was true even when it came to languages, sign included.

"Hurry up, bitch," he whispered, moving in until he was practically touching me. I had to fight not to shy away. I didn't need the reminder, didn't need him to touch me, threaten me again or show me the gun he'd tucked inside his jacket.

He had my parents.

I fumbled with the card as I pulled it out of the ATM and grabbed the cash.

Two hundred dollars. All I could get from the ATM with the limit. He looked at it in disgust but didn't take it from me. He wouldn't. Not here out on the sidewalk, with people passing all around us.

He'd wait.

I shot another look at the camera.

Please. Help.

If somebody didn't figure it out soon...I swallowed as he caught my arm and started to pull me along with him. It was subtle, the way he did it. Anybody looking at us wouldn't figure it out right away. You'd have to really be watching to see it.

I swallowed, my tongue thick and dry in my mouth, my legs wobbly from almost a week with next to no food, hardly any water. He was moving too fast and I could barely keep up. My head spun and everything seemed to blur around me.

When I tripped, he jerked me up, his fingers bruising. "What the fuck are you doing?" he demanded.

"I'm sorry...I just..."

Darkness crowded the edge of my vision.

My knees hurt as I hit the ground, but I didn't even register that I'd done it until a minute later.

"You little—"

"Freeze!"

His eyes came back to me. His voice was a low, ugly whisper. "You just killed them. Bitch. Stupid bitch."

I swallowed. Would have cried, except there were no tears left. None at all.

———◆———

I CAME AWAKE THEN, a knot swelling in my chest. But my eyes, just like that moment, frozen in time, were painfully dry.

These dreams weren't like normal dreams. Not like normal nightmares. I'd rather be chased by a maniacal clown, find myself naked in front of a boardroom with only the annual report in my hand. I'd even go back to the dreams about Drake—those dreams I'd wanted so badly to forget, the ones where I woke up, aching all over. Aching for his touch while my heart cried out for him. Just him.

Even the *other* dreams. The dreams where I was trapped. Wrapped in darkness, and just trapped, while I heard a familiar voice in my ear. *Scream...scream for me.* I'd take any of those, every night for the rest of my life if it meant I'd never have to dream about that final day again.

Too bad it didn't work that way.

There was a faint, rhythmic ticking. Now that I was aware of it, it seemed to grow louder, and louder. Turning my head, I grabbed the watch I'd taken to wearing.

Five a.m. I wouldn't sleep any more. But the thought of dragging my miserable, tired ass out of the bed was more than I could handle. So I lay there, huddled and brooding under the blankets.

It was one thing I did very, very well.

Ten years.

My father had been gone for ten years.

It was supposed to get easier, wasn't it?

Rolling onto my belly, I pressed my face into the pillow as the loneliness, a miserable ache in my gut, just spread and spread.

The minutes bled away into hours, heralded by each slow tick of my watch. I lay there until it was nearly seven, then I forced myself out of bed, showered, packed up the few things I'd brought into the hotel.

It was time to do what I'd come for.

After this, I had no idea what I'd do next.

After ten years, I had faced down the dragon who had haunted my memories...Drake. Not much of a dragon, really. Over the past few weeks, I'd accepted that he wasn't the monster I'd made him out to be. He was the first man I'd ever loved, possibly the only man I'd ever love. My heart still went *bump* when I thought of him and if I'd hoped to exorcise him from my thoughts, from my soul, from my heart, I'd been fooling myself.

Now I had to live with the memory of his hands on me, and the memory of what a fool I'd been. So many years spent blaming him.

True enough, we wouldn't have had the money if Gallagher Enterprises hadn't bought our hotel. My father would still be alive.

But only two men were responsible for locking us up those long miserable days, for every mark they'd left on my mother, every bruise, every broken bone they'd given my father. They were responsible for the bruised kidneys I'd suffered and they were responsible for my nightmares.

Those two men were the ones responsible for my father's death.

All for money. They'd heard my father talking about the money. My dad, naïve, trusting, amazing man that he was, suckered into a card game and he'd been drunk— laughing when one of the men said they'd take him for everything he had with him, even the shirt off his back. Dad had thought it was hilarious. *I got more money now than I know what to do with...you need my shirt? Have it.*

A few foolish words, a card game.

And two cruel men.

Those men were to blame. Not Drake.

And, I realized, not me.

For ten years I'd drifted, unable to figure out who I was, what I was.

I still didn't have any answers. Just more questions. Like...where was I supposed to go from here? What was I supposed to do now?

But I no longer had a *Drake*-shaped object blocking me when I tried to look down the road to my future.

What really blocked me was myself.

———⟡———

IT WAS NINE A.M. WHEN I entered the garden of stone. This was what drew me back here.

The heels of my boots rang hollowly on the carefully laid walkway. I didn't look left nor right, didn't need to search for landmarks. I knew where I was going. Even though I only came here on this day, every year, I could walk this path in my sleep.

Once I found it, my heart stuttered in my chest and I had to pause before I approached.

Images rose up, slammed into me—bright light searing my eyes, voices too loud, one of them louder than all the rest.

Crying—she was crying—why was Mom crying?

Kneeling down, I brushed a few stray leaves, brilliant with color, from my father's grave.

"Hi, Daddy."

The only answer was the whisper of the breeze.

I didn't really expect an answer, though.

How could it have been ten years?

In my pocket was a letter from the prosecutor. One of them was up for parole. Next week. I'd go to the hearing, of course. There really wasn't a question of that. As long as I had a chance in stopping his release, I'd go. I'd say my part. I'd hope to keep him in jail for every second of his sentence.

I could remember that son of a bitch in court, tearfully staring out at the jury. None of this was supposed to happen. We didn't plan to hurt anybody. We just wanted the money. He made it out like it was right there, but we kept having to change up the plan and it got so messed up. I'm so sorry. I ruined people's lives. I'm so sorry.

He ruined people's lives.

And he was sorry.

I thought of his words, so empty and meaningless, a thousand times.

They'd wanted the money—the money my parents had recently received from Gallagher Enterprises. My father, the foolish, hopeful, optimistic dreamer, had been sitting in a bar in Destin, Florida. We were there on a *vacation*, as my parents had put it, but they were talking about moving there. *Someplace warm and sunny. Wouldn't that be nice, Shan?*

Sniffling, I brushed away the tears and focused on the bright spray of flowers that decorated his grave. "It looks like Mom beat me here. I need to get down there more. I've been thinking maybe I'll head to Virginia for a few days when I leave here. I don't really have any place to go right now. No goals. No plans."

Not a single goal. Not a single plan.

Most of my adult life had been goals and plans. College, which I hadn't started until I was nineteen; I had intended to find a job that would fill the void inside me, but nothing did it.

Then, I focused on Drake Gallagher.

I was convinced that just getting *him* out of my system would do something.

Sitting on the grass, I curled my hand into a fist and pressed it to my forehead. "Daddy, I'm an idiot, you know that?"

My free hand, I sank into the grass on top of his grave. When I'd been a child, after a bad dream, I'd sit on his lap and fist my hand in his shirt and he'd tell me a story to make the fear go away.

Nothing could do that now.

Sometimes, I'd sit with him after dinner and he'd talk about the hotel. It would be mine one day, and the idea had fascinated me. He'd tell me about the dreams he had for the place and somewhere along the way, *his* dreams had become mine as well.

It would be the biggest, the grandest place north of Boston. *Just wait and see, Shan. Just wait and see.*

Losing the hotel had been a blow.

Then two months later, I lost him.

And me. The obsession that had pushed me for so long had blinded me to everything.

I don't even know who I am now. Who I *want* to be. The false confidence that had pushed me through life the past few years was gone.

Sighing, I smoothed my hand down the soft, rich grass that blanketed the grave. "Dad, I wish you were here. I'm so confused. I'm tired. I wish I hadn't been such a brat to you before you died. I wish..." I stopped, thinking about how useless wishes were.

If I could change how I'd treated my father, maybe I could change his death. Change how I'd treated Drake. My heart lurched in my chest and a hollowness spread through me as I thought about how much I wished I could undo the past few months.

"If only I could undo it," I murmured. "Undo a lot of things."

Tipping my head back, I stared at the sky, leaden clouds gathering overhead. The breeze had a cool bite to it while vivid leaves – shades of red and yellow - whipped through the cemetery. "There's no undoing anything, though. Is there?"

I found myself thinking about Drake. Not my father, but Drake. The way I'd felt almost happy, for the first time in ten years. If I'd let myself, maybe I could have really *been* happy. Instead, I was selfish and stupid and blind. Now it was too late.

It all felt so unfinished, but I didn't know what to do.

With a tired sigh, I looked back at my father's headstone and smoothed a hand down the grass.

"Happy birthday," I whispered as I rose to my feet. I rested my hand on the stone, lingered one more moment.

As my hand fell away, a prickle danced along my skin. The very air seemed to change.

I wasn't alone.

My breath caught, heart lurched as I turned; I didn't even have to look. I knew who it would be. Part of me wondered why I even *cared*, except I knew the answer to that.

All those unanswered questions rose back up inside me. Unfinished? Oh, hell yes.

But I definitely hadn't planned on finishing anything *here*.

I'd left everything that wasn't mine behind—the phone, the iPad, the files. I'd had movers put my belongings into storage and I'd paid the landlord for the remaining months on my apartment.

I was out of Philadelphia that very night.

And he had been looking for me, that very night. Not even four hours passed before he had started calling, digging up the cellphone number I'd left when I first applied for the job. I saw his name and hadn't answered. That didn't keep him from texting, or leaving voicemails.

I hadn't responded, not even once. Because I didn't trust myself, I'd deleted the messages without reading them. I didn't listen to my voicemail, either.

He hadn't stopped trying, although the calls went from hourly to daily to weekly.

I'd almost blocked his number, but something wouldn't let me.

My chest started to ache and I realized I'd been holding my breath. I forced myself to breathe again as I stared at him, watching as he took one slow step, then another toward me. The early morning mist twined around his legs, his eyes locked on my face, like he didn't dare look away.

Drake.

He'd found me.

Chapter Two

HE'D FOUND ME.

I suppose I'd expected it to happen, but not here.

Unwilling to face him at the place where I was absolutely at my most vulnerable, I moved away from my father's grave, striding to meet him on the landscaped walkway.

My hands moved into my pockets, curling into fists. Maybe if I kept them there, I'd be less likely to reach for him. I'd missed him, yeah, but I hadn't thought it would feel like *this* to see him, have my heart hammer in my chest while my palms slicked with sweat.

He hadn't called in eight days. Eight days.

There had been no calls in eight days.

Maybe that should have prepared me for this.

But why did he have to show up *here*?

How did he know?

My father had been killed in Florida.

We'd paid to have his body brought here.

Ten years ago, news hadn't travelled in *quite* the same way it did now. The internet had been buzzing, yes, but Myspace had been the thing, not Facebook and Twitter. You didn't hear about a murder in Florida unless it was just something really spectacular.

It had shaken the bedrock of my world, but it hadn't made a ripple in the scheme of things. I'm logical enough to realize that.

The events had taken place over just a few days and it had redefined everything for me, but there was no reason—

He stopped in front of me, his gaze locked on my face.

My heart did that crazy lurch inside my chest, but I ignored it, angling my chin up as I planted a cool smile on my face. Although everything inside me felt shaken and it seemed like the ground had crumbled under my feet, I reached for that calm that I'd felt when I'd been in Philadelphia. It had come easily then, not so much now. Maybe because I realized it had been a mask.

But I could fake it. I *would* fake it. Watching him, I lifted an eyebrow and said, "Well, well, well. Small world."

Seconds ticked away. He said nothing.

Something uncomfortable ticked inside me as those green eyes cut into me, but as those moments stretched out and there was simply silence, I shrugged and attempted to walk past him. I felt the heat of him reaching out to me and I could smell that wild, woodsy scent—

His hand closed around my arm and I gasped as he whirled me around, sending me crashing into his chest.

One hand shoved into my hair, a bit longer now. He tangled his hand in it, tugged my head back. "You left," he muttered. That was all he said before his mouth came crashing down on mine.

I sucked in a breath. To scream, to snarl, to tell him to stop. Something. He couldn't do this. Not here. Not when my father lay under six feet of cold dirt just a few yards away. But then, the kiss softened. One hand came up to cradle my cheek and he lifted his head, a harsh rasp of air escaping him as he mumbled against my mouth, "Shan, damn it. Why did you leave me?"

There was something so confused, almost desperate in his voice.

I had him.

The knowledge bloomed inside me and I knew I'd done what I set out to do. I'd wanted him to suffer, as I had.

I'd hurt so badly after he left me, that foolish, naïve girl that I'd been. I'd set my hopes on a dream and it had smashed, but it was more than just the dream I'd lost. It was everything that happened after.

I *had* him.

The very thing I'd set out to do. And it hurt me more than I could even begin to describe. It made me feel dirty, small and evil. The thought of making *him* feel the way I'd felt was enough to make me want to vomit.

Swallowing back the nasty, bitter taste that rose in the back of my throat, I shook my head and disengaged myself from his arms. "Let me go," I said, forcing the words out. I had to get away from here.

I had to get away from *him*.

Had to think.

"Damn it, Shan. We're going to talk," he said, taking a step and advancing on me.

"Not here." I shook my head, looking around, my gaze bouncing off the headstones, the grave markers. Some of them were so old, they were starting to crumble. Slate didn't hold up to the elements very well. Those older ones had stood here in the cemetery for hundreds of years and you couldn't even read them anymore. One held a grinning skull and I stared at its morbid face, hunching my shoulders. "We can't talk here."

"Then where?" he snapped and the heat of his gaze all but scorched me. "In case you haven't noticed, you aren't exactly taking my calls. And you *left*. Is that how seriously you take a job? You just up and leave?"

A *job*. I wanted to laugh, but the jab had its effect. It was a slap to my pride and he likely knew it. "I left a list of qualified applicants with Mr. Coltrane," I said woodenly. "As you probably know, that's not the sort of job I'm cut out for. That fact was driven home once you left and I had time to think. I figured a clean break was best, and Mr. Coltrane had his own administrative assistant."

He scoffed. "Tally doesn't know my company. *You* do. It took nearly three weeks to get things back to where we needed and Mai had to help out. If your intention was to fuck with me, congratulations, you succeeded."

I slid him a look, refused to let him see that his comment had been a direct hit. "Oh, I'm sorry. Did I cost Gallagher Enterprises some money? How thoughtless of me."

"Is that what this is about? You want to get back at me for how I handled everything before? Fine. You did. Slate is clean and we can start over."

I fought the urge to look back over my shoulder. *Slate is clean?* Instead of glancing toward my father's resting place, I shrugged. "If you want to call the slate clean, then we can do that. As to the rest of it?" I shook my head. I couldn't even begin to think about the rest of that now. Not here, of all places.

The thought of starting over with Drake—even for the brief seconds I let myself consider it, had something fluttering to life inside me. It might have been hope, but I crushed it before it could start to grow.

"If you'll excuse me, I have to go."

He blocked my way, his hand coming up to touch my cheek. I averted my face and his hand fell away.

"No starting over?" he said, his voice quiet. "So what was going on between us in Philadelphia?"

"Drake, Philadelphia was..." I didn't know how to answer that. I had to answer him, and if I was wise, if I had any sense of responsibility, I'd give him a *real* answer. But how did I explain that? "Look, this isn't the place to talk about it."

"Then where is? Name the place. The time. Convince me you'll be there and you can walk away."

His eyes were intent on my face.

Name the place. The time. My heart thudded so heavy and hard in my chest and I backed away as he took another step closer. Swallowing, I jerked my head around. "Drake, just..."

"You don't plan on telling me anything," he muttered, shaking his head. "Fine. Here it is. What in the hell happened in Philadelphia, Shan? Explain it to me and I'll go."

My hands shook. I tightened them into fists. *Go?* I didn't know if I wanted him to do that, but I couldn't think. Not here. Not now. "Philadelphia was..." I looked away. "Ten years."

I was babbling, I knew it, but I couldn't stop it. "I had you in my system for ten years and I needed it to stop. I'd always wondered and now I don't have to—"

"That was just..." I paused, then shrugged. "Getting you out of my system. I can't look forward when I'm always looking back and wondering. Now I can stop wondering." I darted a look at him, saw the rigid set of his jaw.

What are you doing? my head screeched at me and my mouth continued to move and I found myself shrugging. "Maybe I should say thanks."

Shut up, shut up, shut up, you idiot! I was horrified. What was I saying? Spinning away, I started to edge around him. I had to get out of there before I made this any worse.

"Look, we can...I dunno. Talk. I'm staying at the—"

I glanced back, pausing by one of the obelisks, those strange memorials that jutted up into the sky. Such an odd way to memorialize the dead. I looked for Drake. He wasn't there. I couldn't see...

Oh.

Oh, no.

Nerves spurred me to move faster as the rain started to come down. "Shannon."

His voice soft, shaken, came from behind me, but I didn't look back.

"For pity's sake, would you—"

I slipped, my heel sliding off the wet stones.

Brilliant pain burst through me as my head struck one of the stones. I heard a shout. It might have been him. It could have been me.

Everything grayed around me and then I caught a glimpse of his face. It was the last thing I saw. Then it was just...darkness.

LIGHTS, BRILLIANT AND blinding, were the first thing I saw...then again, his face.

I barely had a moment to focus on him before everything else assaulted me. The smell hit me first and it was like a fist around my throat.

It took me back, straight back into the hell of that day.

A nurse reached out to touch me and I flung out a fist. Somebody caught my hand and distantly, I heard him speaking, heard the shock in his voice, but nothing connected.

I was too busy hearing the voices from long ago. My mother, saying my name over and over, and my own voice. Screaming. Just screaming. They had just told me—

"Damn it, just back off for a fucking minute!"

Drake's voice cut through everything else and then his hands cupped my face. Sucking in a breath, I stared into his face. His nose was just an inch from mine. My head pounded, throbbed horribly.

Hospital...

I was in a hospital.

I couldn't stand hospitals.

"Why am I here?" I whispered, locking on his face so I didn't have to see anything else.

For a moment, he didn't say anything. He looked at me like I was a stranger and then, slowly, so very slowly, he eased back. "You fell," he said, spacing each word out. "You hit your head."

That might explain the pounding.

It didn't matter. Unless I was in danger of losing a limb or ready to have a heart attack, I couldn't stay here.

Deep inside, I started to tremble and soon, I was shaking so hard, I thought I might be ill. Carefully, I pulled back and Drake reluctantly let go. It took some fumbling but I managed to swing my legs over the edge of the bed. Whoa. Was the floor really that far down?

Doesn't matter—

"Ms. Crosby, you need to—"

A hand went to touch my arm and I jerked my head. Immediately, a thousand slivers of pain sliced into me. I ignored them, focusing on the nurse in front of me. There were three of them, but since they all looked the same, I assumed it was because of whatever I'd done to my head. Focusing on the one in the middle, I waited until my vision settled a bit and then I said softly, "Do not touch me."

"You shouldn't get up," she said, her gaze just as hard as I suspected mine was. "You have a concussion. You're likely to experience some dizziness with the head wound so you need to be still until we've done the assessment. We need to—"

"I am leaving," I said slowly, saying it with great care so she understood me. "I don't care if the doctor wants to run tests or poke or prod. I am leaving and if you don't like it, I don't give a flying fuck."

The lines around her eyes tightened and she inclined her head. "You understand it's dangerous to leave without knowing how extensive your injury is."

"Bite me."

"I'll notify the doctor that you wish to leave."

"I'm not waiting."

Her nostrils flared out a bit and I had a feeling she knew exactly what thoughts were running through my head. "There are forms you'll have to sign if you leave against medical advice."

Yeah. Right. She couldn't make me sign them if I wasn't here when she came back.

"Sure. You go dig them right up." All I had to do was get my feet underneath me.

And figure out how to get Drake out of my way.

His hands caught my shoulders as I went to stand up. Glaring at him, I said, "I have to get out of here."

The longer I stayed here, the harder the memories slammed into me and the worse the feeling of panic, helplessness hit me. A band constricted around my chest and I couldn't breathe.

"Shannon," he said, his fingers hot against my icy flesh. "You're hurt—"

"Listen to me." I cut him off. He had to understand. Had to. "I can't stay here. Please." I reached up, touched his cheek.

His lashes flickered. Then he sighed and looked away. "I'm going to regret this."

But he nodded, reaching up to cover my hand with his own. "Don't leave. You got it? If you try to leave on your own, you'll collapse and just end up back here."

Well, there was that possibility. "Will you get me out of here?" I asked, panic swelling inside me.

"If you'll wait for me. Just...just give me a few minutes." His eyes all but begged me to trust him.

For some reason, I actually *did*. The band around my chest loosened. Oxygen rushed back into my lungs. The pain in my head started to cloud everything— including my ability to think— I heard his voice cutting through everything else.

"I want to talk to her doctor," he said.

The nurse murmured something. I didn't quite catch it.

"I don't care. Get him in here."

———————◆———————

A HAND SHOOK MY SHOULDER. I turned away from it and mumbled under my breath.

Drake persisted and I popped one eye open. Focusing on him hurt. "Go to hell."

"Sure. After you tell me how many fingers."

In response, I lifted one of mine.

A faint smile curved his lips. That smile made my heart flutter as he reached up to brush my hair back. "We did that. And then you disappeared. It took me this long to catch up to you and look how it's turning out. I think we should get some stuff settled before we try it again."

Despite everything, my belly went hot with hunger at the look in his eyes.

Averting mine, I stared at the wall. "Maybe there is no *again*. I told you I probably just needed to get you out of my system."

"Is that a fact?" He touched my lip. "Lucky you, then." His hand lifted again, showed me four fingers. "How many fingers?"

I made a face at him and then sighed. "Four. Now can I sleep?"

"Yes." His hand cradled my cheek. That really shouldn't feel so good. "Want anything while I'm in here?"

"Aspirin," I muttered.

"Can't. Head injury. The doctor ordered Motrin if you want it."

I debated and then nodded. The bed shifted under him as he rose and the floor creaked as he moved away from me. Settling more comfortably into the bed, I stared at the exposed beams of the ceiling over my head. They were a soft, golden wood. Lovely, I had to admit.

I wasn't going to be able to go back to sleep, I realized, lying there waiting for him.

Vague memories of him coming to me in the night, waking me and insisting I count his fingers, tell him my name, surfaced and I turned my head wondering what time it was.

There was a lovely, ornate clock, surrounded by twisting iron scrollwork on one wall.

And the view...

My gut twisted and my heart stuttered.

Slowly, I sat up, staring outside.

I knew that view.

The door opened behind me.

Without turning to look at him, I continued to stare out over the pounding surf.

It was all I could see, the sky a slate gray, the waters churned up as they pounded onto the beach.

I'd seen that view, almost every day, for the nearly the first eighteen years of my life.

My heart slammed against my palm. Odd. I hadn't even realized I reached up to cover my chest. Weird...so weird.

"Where are we?" I asked, my voice wooden, my eyes dry as stone.

"Winsome Cove."

It was like a sledgehammer, right to the heart.

Winsome Cove.

That was the name I'd given this place, back when I'd thought it would be mine. Back when I could still dream about it. Silly daydreams about what I'd do when I inherited the hotel, if I happened to have a few million dollars and could do whatever I wanted.

Gallagher Enterprises had a different plan in mind.

They had sleek, sharp angles, shining glass and bold colors in mind, something sophisticated, to draw the tourists looking for something close to Boston. They weren't looking for *homey* or *quaint*. I'd heard those very words as he spoke to my father, a meeting I wasn't meant to hear.

It was our land they'd wanted, nothing else.

"You son of a bitch," I said, rising from the bed and moving to the window.

Behind me, Drake was silent.

The pounding in my head increased and my knees were wobbly, almost weak.

It didn't get any better. As I moved, my view improved. What I saw spoke nothing of sleek angles or bold colors. There was glass, though, and I could picture how it would gleam under the brilliant light of the sun. The windows ran from roof to floor, facing out over the beach so families could enjoy the view, early in the morning, late at night, whichever they chose.

My heart stuttered, clenched. Then it started to ache in a way that I couldn't even describe.

What was this...?

To the left, there was a balcony and I turned toward it, almost mesmerized. Fumbling with the latch on the French doors, I moved through them and the scent of the saltwater breeze pulled at something deep inside me.

The little alcove had hidden this view from me and I realized we were tucked away, this cottage a little more private. The rest of them were closer together, but each cottage had its own balcony, with doors that opened to the beach, pretty little stone paths that ended at the edge of the sand.

Just as I'd imagined.

"What is this?" I asked, my voice rough.

He didn't answer.

Turning, I stared at him.

He stood with his head bent, staring at the floor.

Wearing battered jeans and a faded T-shirt, he held an orange prescription bottle in his hand but he didn't seem to remember it as he slowly lifted his head to stare at me.

But there was still no answer.

"Damn it, what in the hell is this!" I shouted it at him, the words ripping out of me while the agony inside my head kicked up.

"It's what you wanted," he said softly.

Then he put the bottle down on the little table sitting in front of the window.

Without saying anything else, he left me alone in that wide open room, the soft gray light coming in through the window.

Chapter Three

"STUPID BITCH—"

Pain burst through me. Pain. Shock. I was on the ground. How?

Then hands, dragging me up.

"They're dead. You know that?"

His eyes, narrowed to slits, full of hate and fear, glared down at me as his hand squeezed my face.

Panic burst inside me. I swung out, remembered something my dad had told me. Eyes, baby, he'd said. Go for the eyes.

Then he was screaming and I was running.

Down an alley and that was when I saw them.

Police.

"No!"

SUCKING IN A BREATH, I jerked into wakefulness.

I'd fallen asleep, slumped on the edge of the bed and staring outside.

Night was coming, sunset falling across the ocean like a curtain of gold and fire. The clouds had cleared and my heart burned at the familiar sight. It was almost enough to chase away the dark, heavy feel of the nightmare.

Part of me wanted to just hide in this room for a little while longer. A few hours. The rest of the night. A week at the most. That might let me get a grip, figure out just what was going on.

The nightmare continued to cling, ugly little wisps of it sticking to me like a spider's web. Pushing my hair back, I rose from the bed and looked around. It was the first time I'd really looked around the room.

Bright and open, the walls a soft ivory, the furnishings a pale gold. The focus of the room was the view, the splendid view of the Atlantic.

It's what you wanted.

Closing my eyes, I fought to shove that out of my mind.

Easier said than done.

I wasn't going to be able to quit thinking about it until I *understood*.

Which wasn't going to happen if I stayed in this room. Not for a week, not for the rest of the night. Even a few more hours seemed like too much. The four walls threatened to close in around me and the gloom from the coming darkness was thick. Hitting a light pushed the shadows back, but it did nothing to dispel the weight that threatened to crush me.

I recognized the feeling.

That sense of dread had chased me for months, years after I'd left and it had taken me years to shake it off completely. I wasn't going to let it pull me down again.

All of this was supposed to *free* me of my past, not drag me down further.

I headed toward the door, practically desperate for escape, but halfway there, I passed by the mirror and the sight of the woman there made me pause.

Going still, I faced her, saw the pallor, the shadows under her eyes.

Sighing, I closed the distance and reached up, touched the reflection. "I thought I'd buried you," I murmured.

It was a shattering revelation, standing there and realizing I could still see her. Still see echoes of the scared, tired girl I'd been ten years ago. Oh, I *looked* older and the naiveté was gone. But the fear, the vulnerability was still there. That uncertainty and lack of confidence. Naïve, no. I wasn't that. But I was still unsure. I looked like the timid girl the police had pulled off the streets that day.

I looked like a victim.

It wasn't acceptable.

Curling my hands over the edge of the hand-carved bureau, I breathed, held it. Took another, slow, steadying breath. You aren't who you used to be. A few bad dreams, a knock on the head, that's not enough to send you back there, Shannon.

My head throbbed, pain emanating from a spot just above my right ear, but I ignored it, focusing on the way air moved in and out of my lungs, the soothing lull of my own heartbeat. After a few minutes, I felt steadier. Almost calm.

When I looked back at my reflection, I looked almost like myself again.

Tired, yes.

But I could live with tired.

I'd just had the sense knocked out of me. *Tired* was acceptable.

Weak wasn't.

———— ◉ ————

THE LIGHTS WERE LOW when I opened the door.

But I had no trouble seeing him.

He sat before a slow-burning fireplace, the glow from his MacBook casting light on his face, while the fire cast amber glints off the whiskey gleaming in the glass a few inches from his hand.

He wasn't working, though.

He sat there, just staring at the fire.

Until he heard me, that is.

Then he turned his head, his lashes low, shielding his gaze from me.

He reached out a hand, caught the glass and I watched as he lifted it to his lips. His throat worked and it was just insanity that I still wanted to go to him and press my lips to the strong muscles there. My mouth watered just thinking about it.

He put the glass down and looked away, focusing on the MacBook with an intensity that would have completely fooled me had I not seen him staring at the fire blankly just a moment before.

"How's your head?" he asked.

"Sore." I moved a little farther into the room, looking around. The place was huge, practically the size of the condo I'd been renting in Philadelphia. Off to the side, I caught a glimpse of the kitchen, lost in shadows. "You haven't been in to make me practice my counting skills."

His hands stilled on the laptop, then he shrugged. "It's been twenty-four hours."

"Twenty..." I blinked, freezing in my tracks as I did the math. It was completely over, then. I'd hit my head and slept through the final hours of the anniversary. Turning away, I pressed my lips together while tears burned my eyes. The ache in my throat was massive, like I'd swallowed a boulder. "I need to call my mother."

"She's called you."

Slowly, dread curdling inside me, I turned back to him and watched as he reached out a finger, nudging the phone toward the edge of the table where he worked. "I let it go to voicemail the first few times, but then she started calling every hour, thought she might be worrying so I took the call. Told her you'd hurt your head and I was just watching you while you got some sleep."

A fist grabbed my throat.

"Did you..." Oh, no. This...This was bad. "Did she ask who you were?"

"Yes. I told her my name was Mike, that I was a friend of yours. She accepted it."

"Mike..." The relief slammed into me and I sagged, collapsing on the low chair a few feet from the couch. "Michael—that's your middle name."

He didn't respond. His expression was like stone as he focused back on whatever he had been working on.

I fought the urge to apologize. I'd left him in the lurch. I was a selfish bitch, and I knew it.

Guilt and shame knotted inside me and I wrapped my arms around my middle as it all twisted and stormed inside me.

A hand touched my knee and I looked up as he wrapped a blanket around me. "You're shaking," he said softly.

"Am I?"

My teeth were chattering. Distantly, that struck me as odd. I wasn't cold—was I?

He went to turn away and I reached out a hand, catching his arm.

"Sit with me," I said, the words coming out before I even knew what I wanted.

I didn't want to be alone.

Alone, as I'd been for so many years. Mom and I had tried to pull each other through, but I'd blamed myself, she'd blamed herself, and then...we'd drifted. Eventually, she started to heal, but I just stayed where I was.

Alone. Lonely. Miserable...and deep inside, the anger grew.

Only I'd focused it on the wrong person.

As Drake reached up and brushed my hair back, I stared at him.

"I don't think that's wise," he said, softly.

"Why not?"

"Because there's too much we haven't said to each other."

Licking my lips, I fumbled for a smile. It felt fake, awkward on my face. "I...I just want to sit here. I'm not up for anything else."

"That's just it. You're not up for anything else, and that's what I want." His hand slid down, curved around my neck and I froze as he moved in, pressed his lips to my brow. That pounding that had gripped me, nauseating me every time I woke up faded, eased, under just that light touch. "I want everything from you, Shannon. I'm not talking about now. You're hurt and I know that. But in general? Yeah. I want everything. I always have. Ten years didn't change that. You walking away didn't change that. But you're angry with me, you're keeping secrets and once you heal up, you'll walk out that door again...won't you?"

Oxygen seemed to die inside me. Barely able to breathe, I sat there, watching him. His thumb stroked down my neck, rubbing over my skin in a gentle caress.

"I..." I licked my lips. "I don't know, Drake. I don't know what I want, or what I want to do. I can't answer that."

He nodded and then rose, moving back to the couch.

"I'm sorry," I whispered.

His eyes closed and then he dropped his face into his hands.

A moment later, he surged off the couch and started to pace.

"Don't."

The word, bitten off like he was chewing glass, caught me off guard.

I sucked in a breath, staring at him as he stopped in his tracks and turned to stare at me. The green of his eyes all but glowed. "Don't you fucking apologize to me. I don't want to hear it."

"I..." I stopped, snapping my jaw shut as words jumbled and caught inside my throat. "Okay. What *do* you want me to say?"

He opened his mouth, closed it. Then turned away, staring at the wall. Under the fine material of his shirt, I could see how his muscles tightened and bunched, like he had to fight to remain still, just to stand there.

"Drake?"

I couldn't even explain it, but dread curled inside me as he slowly turned around and stared at me.

"Tell me," he said, his voice frozen, artic.

I swallowed, my hand tightening in the blanket. "Tell you what?"

Even before he said it, I knew.

"Tell me about Florida."

THE VIRGIN

*"WHAT THE FUCK DO YOU mean, you don't have the money here?"
he roared, lifting a hand.*

I stuffed a fist against my mouth, determined not to scream. Every other time I'd screamed, they'd struck out. Not at me, though. They always hit my dad—or my mom. They didn't leave marks on her, but they'd hit her in the stomach, used their belts on her thighs. Anything to hurt her in places that couldn't be seen.

Dad, though, he was so battered, I couldn't even recognize him. Except for his eyes. Those wide gray eyes, just like mine. Before this had happened, those gray eyes were usually absent as he thought about this daydream, or that. Or they'd gleam with humor. Now they were stark, with fury or fear, as he watched the two men who were likely to kill us all.

The man brought his hand across my father's face and I let myself scream—in my head. Aloud, I didn't make a sound and I stared into the eyes of the man who had come over to watch me, smiling just a little like he hoped I would cry. He liked it when I did because he liked to hit my father just so I'd beg him not to. As I fought to silence it, he crouched down and looked at me. "Come on. Scream, little girl. Just once."

I stared into his eyes, terrified. And I bit the inside of my cheek until it bled. I wouldn't scream, not again. I ached all over and something low in my back hurt—I'd never hurt like that before. But I wouldn't scream.

The other man just stood in front of Dad, his chest heaving, his eyes bright with rage. "You stupid shit. You got money. We heard you bragging about it and we did some digging around. You sold some piece of shit hotel for two million dollars. Why the fuck can't you get it?"

"Our bank is in Boston," Mom said, her voice cool, almost scathing...but not quite there. My throat closed up as I looked at her, pride flooding me, love swamping me. She was so beautiful, so brave. Twice that man had started to hit me and she'd drawn his attention—he'd attacked her instead and I'd crouched on the floor, hating myself for making him want to hit me, and for Mom taking the blows instead.

He never left a mark on me. My stomach hurt from how many times he'd pummeled me, how many times he'd jabbed a fist into my side.

I hurt all over. Mom...I swallowed the moan in my throat and forced myself to be quiet. If she could do this, I could. Stonily, I watched as she raked her eyes over him, like he was something nasty she'd found on the doorstep. "We can get money from the ATM, but if you want a lot of money, we'd have to get it wired."

"Then tell me how to do that." The first man—his name was Peter, I think—came over to her, smiling a little. It was like he wanted her to help him out. He'd told us that. Help me out, I'll let you go. But he wouldn't. I knew that. If he let us go, we'd go to the cops. He'd have to kill us. "Tell me what to do and we'll wire the money down."

"You can't." My mother tipped her head back, staring up at the ceiling. "It has to be my husband and me. It's a joint account and anything over a certain amount requires both of us to be present." She gave them a thin smile. "I put that precaution in place because my husband is notoriously bad with money."

She was lying...

I flinched as Peter started to yell.

The other one swore and went to my father, a hand lifted. But Peter caught him. "Stop it! We gotta think. If she's telling the truth and we need both of them, he can't go in there looking like that."

"Yeah, yeah. We need money now, though."

His eyes came to me, an appraising look in his face.

My skin started to crawl.

———◦———

JERKING MYSELF OUT of that hellhole of memories, I sucked in a breath and turned away. My legs were wooden and moving felt impossible. I managed to move the few feet to the chair, but that was it. Slowly, I sank down and stared at the fire, watching as the flames danced, flickered. "What do you mean, what happened?" I asked softly.

"Your father was murdered."

A second later, a tablet was tossed down on the leather ottoman in front of me. I knew the article. It was one of the many that had plastered the newspapers for several days after we were rescued. *Bittersweet end to tragedy. Father killed. Mother and daughter rescued from kidnappers.*

Bittersweet end. They thought that touched on it.

There was no mention of my name. My mother had fought, tooth and nail, to keep my name from being mentioned. Since I hadn't officially turned eighteen yet, she managed to win, but just barely.

I reached out and touched a fingertip to my father's image, there in the article. They lauded him as a hero, him and Mom. A few people did figure out who I was, but I'd left as soon as I was able, going back only for the hearings and the trial. The men accepted a deal from the DA and I still refused to talk, so the reporters moved on to greener pastures.

"Every time I cried, they hit him." The words slipped out of me before I realized I was going to say anything.

A shadow fell across my hand and I looked up as Drake sank down in the chair across from me, his face so rigid, it could have been cut from stone. Looking back down at my father's face, I swallowed. "If I screamed, if I didn't do what they asked, they beat him, or they'd hurt Mom. They never left marks on her face, but they had other ways of hurting her. Punching her in the belly, using a belt on her legs. Anything to hurt her, and they'd watch me, let me know it was my fault. They hit me some, especially at first, but it was always in the belly—like they didn't want to leave any bruises or anything. They loved to hurt my parents, though, no matter what I did, no matter how quiet I was.

I learned fast not to do anything. Not to say anything. And to do what they wanted."

"They wanted money."

I nodded. "Dad had been...well, talking. They didn't know all of his money was in a bank in Boston and it wasn't like he could make a huge withdrawal out of an ATM." I shrugged and pulled my hand back, curling it in a fist and tucking it inside the blanket. That cold chill had settled inside me again. Frozen. I felt frozen solid. "But they needed money immediately...they had people breathing down their necks for something. Once a day, they dragged me to an ATM. That's why they never hit my face. They didn't want the attention. I'd go to the ATM and when I was there, in front of those little cameras, I'd sign out *Help. Please.*" Absently, I signed it out as I spoke, staring off at nothing. "My grandmother was deaf. That's how I knew sign, although I'd forgotten most of it. One of the security guards had seen it. Figured out what I was doing and called the cops. The men who grabbed us had been waiting until Dad healed up enough—Mom had told them that they would need a wire transfer. She'd convinced them that they couldn't get the money any other way and that they'd need both of them present to make the transfer. Dad was so messed up, he couldn't go anywhere without attracting attention. But they kept taking me to the ATM."

I rubbed my hand down my thigh, trying to warm myself as I talked. "That last day, I signed again. We were about to leave. I tripped and fell. I was tired. Hungry. Hadn't eaten in days. It's a blur, what happened. There were cops. Before I fell? After? He told me that I'd killed my parents and..."

I stopped, shook my head.

Rising, I moved over to the window, staring outside.

"He had a radio. I remember hearing him shout through it. I heard my mom. Heard her say my name. She told me to run. My dad—his voice." I had to stop, leaning forward, pressing my head against the window as I waited for the ache in my throat to ease up, so I could get the rest of it out. "He said he loved me. Then..." I licked my lips. "The guy who had taken me out—his name was Todd. Todd Young. He jerked me back up, and hit me. I fell again. Everything went blurry but somehow I got to my feet, started to run. He was screaming. Then there were cops everywhere and..."

Heaving out a sigh, I turned and looked at him. "That's it. I don't remember anything until I woke up in the hospital. My mom was there. They'd shot her, but it went in and out. She was crying when I looked at her, holding my hand. They'd killed my dad. As soon as that bastard who took me out called back in, the other one—his name was Peter—turned and looked at my parents. He told them, *You can thank your daughter for this.* Then he lifted the gun. My mom had gotten free, somehow. She rushed him. The bullet went through her side—she lost a kidney, but it hit a window, broke it. Police had already been searching the area and they got there...too late. After he got up, he pointed the gun at my dad and just like that, my father was gone."

Just like that.

Memories slammed into me and it was too much. Unable to take the stillness anymore, unable to take his grim silence, I forced myself to move. One foot in front of the other, until I was in the bedroom. There, I curled up in the middle of the bed and wrapped my arms around my knees.

Just like that.

Chapter Four

CAN'T BREATHE—

Pain exploded through me.

Staring through the tears burning my eyes, I struggled to see. Mom...Dad...

Don't talk, some small voice in the back of my head told me. Brutal hands fisted in my hair, jerked my head back. A voice, ugly and amused, whispered in my ear, Scream, little girl. Scream so I can hurt him.

Not right. Even through the pain, I knew it. That wasn't right.

A hand shoved me to my knees, still holding me tight. Look at him. Look!

Through my tears, I stared. I tried to see him, but—

A light fell across his face just as the second man, Peter, moved up to stand behind him. We'll get out. We'll come after him. And you. Your mother. You'll never be free—

He swung out with a tire iron, the same one he'd used to smash into my father's stomach the very first day they'd grabbed us. And I watched as he smashed it into Drake's head.

Blood exploded, so much blood. It flowed and flowed until it flooded the entire room.

I woke up screaming.

Screaming and trapped in Drake's arms.

Even though his scent cued me in as to who was holding me, panic flooded my body and I swung out.

My elbow caught his throat and I heard the choked noise, dimly, as I scrambled free.

Crouched on the floor, in the middle of the room, light hurting my eyes, my befuddled, confused brain struggling to catch up, I sat there and stared.

Drake, red-faced, struggling to breathe, sat on the edge of the bed and stared right back.

Shame slammed into me. Shame for the weakness, shame for having him see me like this.

I jerked my gaze away from him and rose, my legs shaky, my head pounding. "I'm sorry," I said, forcing the words out.

He was silent. Unable to just stand there, I moved into the bathroom and turned on the water, splashing the icy wet across my face, gasping at the shock of it, welcoming it as it cleared some of the cobwebs from my mind.

There was no sound, but I knew when he came up to stand behind me.

Slowly, I straightened and met his gaze in the mirror. The redness had faded from his face. His voice was a little hoarse as he asked, "How often does this happen?"

"What?" I asked flippantly. "Me elbowing somebody in the throat? Not very."

His mouth flattened out. "The nightmares, Shan."

I took my time reaching for a towel and drying my face, formulating half a dozen answers before finally settling on the truth. With a sigh, I turned and faced him, leaning on the edge of the counter. "Now? Not very. A few times a year, I'll have a really bad one. This time of the year is the worst. The rest of the time, it's just echoes. Sometimes, I'll sleep walk, move around a little and try to hide. Other times, it's just restless sleep. That..." I paused and blew out a breath. "That was a bad one. They used to all be bad ones. I couldn't sleep without taking a sleeping pill. Sometimes, it helped."

I shrugged and looked down at the hand towel I still held, twisting it around in my hands. "But other times, the nightmares would still find me. I couldn't wake up. So I'd be stuck."

He crossed the distance between us, just a few small steps. One hand lifted, came up to cup my cheek. I held still, barely able to breathe as his eyes searched mine.

"I've spent the past two months trying to understand why you ran." His hand slid down, curved around my neck and then he lowered his head, pressed his brow to mine. His lids drooped lower, shielding his eyes, although I could still see a thin rim of green. "And before that, I came here, every summer, waited on that fucking balcony every night for three weeks, just waiting for you. I thought, *she'll be here. One day, she'll be here. She can't stay away from a place she loves like this*. But you never came back, not that I could see. Now I know why."

His hand fell away and he straightened, turning away.

"Why did you really come to Gallagher Enterprises, Shan?" he asked softly. "You have every reason in the world to hate me. Every reason to avoid me. Running, I can understand, but why show up in the first place?"

As he pivoted back around to study me, I ducked my head, staring at my bare feet. Curling my toes into the plush, warm rug that spread out over much of the tiled floor, I debated on that answer. I could lie. I knew how to do it, how to look at a person and lie without blinking, without flinching. When you spent years trapped in a pit of depression that seemed unending, lying became almost second nature.

How are you, Shannon?

I'd smile and nod. I'm getting by. Every day seems to get a little easier.

Are you holding up?

A shrug, a shake of the head. Nothing else you can do. A nervous laugh. It's what Dad would have wanted, right? I'll be okay. Really.

You're looking so much better! You are so brave. Your father would be so proud of you.

Thank you. It means a lot to hear that. A smile, a nod...even as I'm screaming inside, I don't want to make my father proud...I want him here.

Oh, yes. I could lie. I could look Drake right in the eye and offer glib words that would ease this tension, angry words that would push him away. Or I could offer him more half-truths. I *had* wanted to get him out of my system. It hadn't worked.

Now he was in my system, in my soul, in my blood. I could taste him on my lips as I slept, feel his body under my hands in my dreams, and when I woke, sometimes I even imagined I could still smell the scent of his skin on mine.

Feeling the weight of his gaze on my head, I slowly raised my head and stared at him.

In the bright, golden lights of the bathroom, I felt exposed and stripped bare.

The small, scared part of me whispered... Lie. Just lie. It's so much easier. So much safer.

But that was the crux of my problem. I'd felt *safe* in Florida, and look what happened. Since then, there was rarely a day when I truly felt safe. What I *felt* was loneliness, anger, guilt and confusion.

I lived in the shadows and I wrapped myself in lies, just to keep people at bay.

In that moment, I realized how very tired of it all I was.

But the lies, and the shadows, would continue unless I pulled myself out of them.

Blood roared in my ears, my heart pounding in my throat. I rubbed my palms together, felt the sweat that had collected there. Clearing my throat, I looked around. Not here. I wasn't having this talk here. In a bathroom, lush and elegant as it was.

"Let's go out to the balcony," I said softly.

He looked away, his shoulders rising, falling on a rough breath. "It's cold."

"I grew up on these beaches. I know the weather."

He just nodded.

COLD, MAYBE.

But the built-in fire pit, powered by a gas line, chased away most of the chill. Drake wrapped a blanket around my shoulders and I drew my feet up on the cushion, tucking them under me. Between the fire and the blanket, I barely felt the chill in the air.

Not physically.

Inside, I felt chilled to the bone. And sick at heart.

Drake sat across from me, his hands folded, his gaze on the dancing flames. There was no delaying this. Not anymore.

"I hated you," I said softly.

His shoulders tightened, his body going rigid as though he was preparing for a blow. But when he spoke, his voice was cool, the way it might be if he was addressing some of the hotshots back at Gallagher Enterprises. "I can understand why. I just want to understand what's happened the past few months."

He didn't understand.

But then again, neither did I. Not really.

"For the past ten years, I fixated on you. Blaming you." I shrugged and looked away. "I had to delay college until I was nineteen. Mom wishes I'd put it off another year, but I was going crazy. She..." I paused, wondering if there was a way to say this without coming off as cruel. "She blamed herself. For a long time. It was their job, she said. To protect me. When I was hurt, it was a failing of hers."

Drake swore, shoving upright. He started to pace, tension coming off him in waves. "None of you were to blame. A couple of sick bastards

135

wanted to hurt you, exploit you, steal from you and your family. The blame lies with them."

"I know."

He paused and looked back at me.

I focused on the fire, stunned by how much lighter I felt, just by saying those words out loud. I'd never been able to do it before, even though I'd told myself I accepted that fact years before. Over the past month especially, I'd been coming to realize just how blind I'd been in my rage toward Drake. Closing my eyes, I pressed my head to the pillowed side of the chair. "It took me a very long time to be able to see that. I blamed myself. I blamed you. I blamed your family."

His gaze cut toward me and I laughed. "Please, Drake. It was *Gallagher Enterprises* that authorized the project...not just you." Sighing, I tipped my head back and stared up at the endless expanse of sky overhead. "I blamed my mother. I blamed the cops for not finding us, not realizing those guys were out there. I blamed the security guards for not realizing what I was saying sooner. And I *did* blame the men who grabbed me. But it took a long time for me to stop blaming everybody else around me, everybody who'd been in my life around that time." I plucked at a loose thread on the blanket, forcing the last of the words out. "Including my father."

The boards under his feet creaked and I looked up, watched as he settled across from me.

"Your father."

"Yes." Tears stung my eyes. Impatient, I dashed them away. "He was the reason we went to Florida. He talked about the money. He trusted too many people and that was the reason he ended up in a bad way to begin with, why we had to sell out anyway. Yes, I blamed him. I blamed you. I blamed everybody."

Clutching the blanket, I stood up and went to the railing and stared out over the water, watching as it crashed into the beach. "Most of all, I blamed myself."

He joined me at the railing, his eyes on the rolling surf. "Why?"

"I lived. He didn't. They battered him. I had bruised ribs and a bruised kidney. Oh...and skinned knees from where I fell. You couldn't even recognize him when they were done with him." Turning my head, I stared at him, swallowing so I could speak around the knot in my throat. "It's been ten years. And the clearest image I have in my head of my dad is the way he looked that last day, his face bruised and his mouth busted open. Most of those came from the times when I couldn't stop myself from screaming. I can't *see* my father the way I want to. Those are the clearest memories I have of him, no matter what I do. I can't cut those images out of my head."

He moved then, so fast I couldn't even prepare for it. His hands plunged into my hair, tugging my head back until all I could see was his face. "And is that what he'd want? Would he want that to be how you remember him?"

"It doesn't *matter*. I can't get it out of my head! I did that to him. For weeks *before* that happened, I didn't want to talk to him. Not to him, to Mom. I hid in my room, or in the hotel and stared outside, feeling sorry for myself. Because they had done what they could to make sure I'd be taken care of." I curled my lip, glaring at him. "Poor little Shan. Her parents were in the hole so bad. Then a rich guy comes and buys up their hotel. Now we've got lots of money and what am I'm twisted up over? *You*."

I jerked away from him, ignoring the nauseating way my head pitched and rolled.

Stumbling away, I curled my hands over the railing, tried to steady my knees. "I hated *everybody*."

"You had a right to hate me," he said, his voice hard as stone.

"No." I had to get this out. The poison inside me had festered for too long. "A right to be angry...maybe. I still don't understand why you wasted your time with me, but that's neither here nor there. I didn't need to hate your family, my parents, the cops...or myself. I've been trapped for ten years and I'm tired of it."

Unable to stand there any more, I turned away.

He didn't follow me.

I can't decide if I was happy about that or not.

MORNING CAME. TOO BRIGHT, and as far as I was concerned, too early.

Squinting against the light shining through my window, I groaned as the pounding continued inside my head and tried to think about the fact that I had to go out there. Face Drake. Figure out how to get out of this place, figure out what to do next.

At some point in the next few days, I had to make it down to Florida.

Thinking was so hard, though, and the ache in my skull only made it worse.

What do you want to do? That small voice inside my head murmured to me and I closed my eyes.

What did I want?

Slowly, I rolled to an upright position and stared outside, gazing out over the rolling waters. They called to me. The ocean always had. Even the beaches of Florida had beckoned to me, but nothing like it did here.

Home.

What I wanted?

That was easy.

It was this.

This place.

On the rare occasion I had happier dreams, it was of this. On the rare occasion I let myself think about *what-if?* I imagined myself here.

Building something here, making something that mattered. All I'd ever wanted.

I wanted this. I wanted *home*.

And...

An ache settled in my throat.

Drake.

Still.

Always.

It was what you wanted.

This beautiful place, like he'd reached inside me and captured my dreams, brought them to life; he'd done it because I'd wanted it. He'd come back here, hoping to find me. That meant something, didn't it?

Was it foolishness to hope we still had a chance?

Just the thought of it was enough to make my heart race. Enough to make my palms go damp while the yearning swamped me. Every time I'd woken up alone over the years, some part of me had wished for...something. No. Not something. That empty void inside me had a name and only he could fill it.

They say youthful infatuations are fleeting, that they never last.

But mine turned into an obsession...a love that haunted me even now.

A chance.

Sliding off the bed, I moved to stand in front of the mirror, studying my reflection. It hadn't been all that long ago that I had stood in Philly, staring at my reflection critically, wondering if he'd see the girl I'd been under the layers of sophistication I'd developed over the years.

I'd been fooling myself to think that he wouldn't see that girl.

She was still there. Under a thick layer of bitterness, anger and hurt, she was still there. I could see her clearer now. I could even *feel* her. Maybe it was because something had pierced that layer of bitterness.

I could see her—see *me*. Nothing had ever been more clear in that moment, standing in the dark, wearing Drake's button-up shirt and a pair of his boxers that bagged around my waist. Scowling, I looked down at myself, realizing I'd been wearing the same clothes since I'd arrived here—how long had it been? Thirty six hours, maybe?

It seemed about right.

I needed to think. I needed to clear my head. And I really, really needed a shower.

I spent a good twenty minutes under the hot, pounding spray. I came to one conclusion.

It was time. Time to start over. Time to reach for a second chance. Here, back where *everything* had started. Here, with Drake.

Although the water was hot, goosebumps raced across my flesh while my belly clenched. There was a tight, hot knot there and I groaned, leaning back against the tiles. They were heated by the water and their warmth seeped into me, turning my already loose muscles into putty. My breath hitched in my chest and my heartbeat raced.

I wanted to start over.

I wanted a chance with Drake.

Was I going to go do this?

I didn't know.

The thought of it terrified me.

The thought of *not* doing it terrified me more.

It was that thought that pushed me to turn off the water, to reach for one of the towels, hanging on a heated rod. I wrapped it around my body and then grabbed another, drying the water from my hair. My hands were shaking the entire time though. As I dried my hair, as I wrapped the towel around my head, as I finished toweling off and as I slicked some of the lotion I found on the counter over my skin.

Even as I brushed my teeth, I could see how my hands shook. When I finished, I reached for the towel and let my wet hair spill down around my face, using my hand to finger comb through the loose curls, wincing as I felt the lump that had ended up putting me in this predicament.

Once I'd finished, I lowered my hands to the counter and stood there, staring at my reflection.

"Pull yourself together," I said to the woman in the mirror.

Without waiting to see if she took my advice, I adjusted the damp towel back around my torso and turned to the door.

Chapter Five

COOL AIR KISSED MY flesh as I opened the door and moved into the wide open living room. There was a fire roaring in the stone hearth and in front of it, sprawled in a chair was Drake. The golden light from the fire set the deep red of his hair to flame and he was lost in thought, staring into the glass of bourbon he held in front of him.

I stood there, watching as he lifted it, looking down into it without drinking it.

I took a step forward and froze as his gaze cut to me.

It was like the fire in the hearth reached out to lick my flesh. I was flaming hot, and all because he'd looked at me.

The wooden floor under my feet was the only thing that felt cool. Even the air was supercharged, heated against my skin as I took another step, then another. Soon, there was no more steps left to take and I stood in front of him, wearing nothing but the towel, looking down at him while he swirled the whiskey in his glass and then tossed it back. "You should be resting."

"I've done nothing but that for the past day and a half." I reached out, touching the glass with my fingertip. There was barely a swallow left. "Can I?"

He gave it to me, his gaze burning on mine.

I lifted it to my lips and followed his example, tossing it back, relishing the heat as it burned down my throat. I put the glass down on the table next to his chair and then, straightening, I held his gaze and dropped the towel.

His eyes went black.

It was strange, but as I eased in, the nerves that rippled inside me faded. Bracing one knee beside his thigh, I rested a hand on his shoulder and then brought up my other knee. My heart knocked hard against my ribs and need was a scream in my blood. Lifting my other hand up, I slid them along the wall of his chest. My senses felt heightened, too much, so that the nubby fabric of his sweater abraded my palms. The sweater covered hard muscle and I could remember, so vividly, how it had felt to have him pressed against me.

"Shan."

His hands gripped my waist. I could feel the imprint of each finger, the callouses an exquisite torture against my skin. But he didn't pull me closer. He just waited. My breath caught in my throat as he stared at me.

"What are you doing?" he asked, his voice a gruff whisper.

"Doesn't take much to figure out." I pressed my mouth to his. "Not really."

A groan rumbled out of him. His hands tightened. But his lips remained firm, unmoving, under mine. I caught his lower lip between my teeth and tugged. Then, slowly, I lifted my head and rested my brow against his. "I spent ten years alone, miserable with it. I'm tired of it."

His green eyes held mine as I slid my hands down, worked them under the hem of his sweater.

Heated flesh met my palms as I dragged them upward, baring his chest. "I'm tired of wondering. I'm tired of wishing. I'm tired of dreaming. I'm tired of being lonely. I just want to..."

I stopped, biting my lip as the words froze in my throat. Instead of trying to force the words out, I pressed a kiss to his brow. Then the hard, carved line of one cheekbone. The other. I worked my way back to his mouth and said softly, "I want to feel. I'm tired of *not* feeling. You're the only one who ever really made me feel anything."

His hand tangled in my hair and my breath caught as he wrapped it around his fist. "Is that what this is about? You want to feel something?"

"I've always felt something with you." We were so close, I could feel his breath dancing over my lips. I freed a hand and pressed it to his cheek. "Whether it was the way you dazzled me and made me burn inside ten years ago, or the hurt that came after. When I finally stopped hurting, I felt something else. I was mad...so mad." Leaning in, I pressed my lips to his, rubbed them back and forth as a shiver raced down my spine. "I kept telling myself that anger was still there even up until..."

His hand molded over the back of my skull as the words died. I had to clear my throat before I could continue and when I did, I was no longer even sure what I'd started out to say. "I'm tired of existing in the past. I just want to start living again."

I pressed my lips to his.

His fingers tangled almost painfully in my hair and his eyes glinted, sunlight shining through the fog. The only warning I had was the way his body tightened beneath mine. We moved and in a blink, we were flat on the low-lying table that stretched across the floor. His chest crushed me and I reached up, gripping his torso. My heart raced, desire, hunger ripping at me.

Need had vicious claws and it left me breathless. Drake braced one hand by my ear, raising his head to look down at me. "I can make you feel," he rasped. Then he shoved up on his knees and tore his sweater away. He came back and I almost sobbed at the feel of him pressed against me.

A big, hard palm cupped my breast, his thumb circling my nipple.

I felt that—all the way down to my core where I already ached for him. I'd been empty, longing for him, for *this*, ever since I'd walked away.

Desperation roared inside me as he kissed a burning line down my neck to take my nipple in his mouth. At the same time, he cupped me in his hand. I cried out, reaching for him. He pushed two fingers inside me, twisted. "Shan," he muttered.

I panted as he worked me closer and closer to orgasm, something that had been elusive until he'd taken me. Now, I raced toward him and as he sent me flying, just like that, his name echoed inside my mind, although I didn't even have the breath to whisper it.

There was no time to catch my breath, either, because I hadn't even had a chance to drift back down when he started to blaze another hot, open-mouthed trail down my torso, my belly, until he could nuzzle the curls between my thighs. Instinctively, I tensed even as he urged my thighs wider apart. "Feel this," he said against my flesh, the caress of air against me another teasing torment.

Then he licked me, bold and demanding, stabbing at my clit while I twisted and shuddered. Beneath my back, the table was hard and unyielding. Against me, Drake was every bit as hard, and he wasn't much more yielding than the wood, but those kisses...hot, hungry kisses against my pussy, his tongue taunting my flesh until I was arching up to meet each teasing flick.

Nothing else seemed to exist. Just the flickering flames as they danced across our skin, and his hands holding me tight as he worked his torturous magic on me.

I loved it, and I hated it because it wasn't enough.

I reached down and fisted my hands in his hair, pulled insistently. Demands fought to form in my throat, but I couldn't get anything out except, "You."

He caught my clit between his teeth and tugged, humming against my swollen flesh.

"Drake, damn it...I want *you*."

"You have me."

Snarling, I twisted and arched against him and he laughed, started his way back up my body.

"You want to feel," he said, bracing his weight above me. There was no laughter in his eyes now and his gaze was hot, molten. Quicksilver. "Feel what I've felt. Desperate. Frustrated. Dying for what you think you can never have."

Stroking my hands down his chest, I toyed with the button of his jeans. "So I can't have you?"

Under my hands, I felt the heavy column of his cock and yearning flooded me, wrapped itself around me. If he pulled away, I might cry. I might break. I might throw myself at him and beg—

"You can have whatever you want."

I freed the button and fought with the zipper until I managed to drag it down over his length. "I want this," I said once I'd freed him. Wrapping my hand around him, I stroked him, fumbling until I caught the rhythm and watched his eyes go opaque. "I want to feel you inside me. Now."

He reached down and caught my hand, pinned it down by my head, pressed it there. "Now."

The blunt tip of his cock probed between my thighs and I shifted, my breath catching as he slowly pushed inside. "Do you feel me now?" he demanded.

Twisting my hips, I tried to take him deeper. "Yes..." I groaned, closed my eyes. "More. Please."

Instead, he withdrew until we were just barely connected. My eyes flew open and I stared up at him. "Drake."

"Watch me. See me. I want to see you come apart, see you as I fill you."

The rough, velvet timbre of his voice was another caress and I shuddered all over again as he started to push inside me. Again, he stopped without filling me, withdrawing and holding there, watching me. I tightened my grasp on his hand, digging my nails into his skin in desperation. He was going to drive me crazy—"Oh!"

He drove in hard, fast, deep. The sound of my cry bounced off the walls and then he did it again and again, while I lay there, open and helpless, craving every deep, ruthless twist of his hips. "Feel me," he snarled, bending down to catch my mouth in a deep, drugging kiss. "Have me."

His mouth left mine to kiss a burning path down my neck and there, at the curve where neck met shoulder, he sank his teeth in, sucking hard and fast, a delicious little suction that added another sensation to my already overloaded system.

He let go of my hand and shifted his grip, moving to hook my thighs over his elbows. I felt almost bruised from him now as he sank so deeply inside me. "Say my name," he muttered against my ear.

"Drake." It stuttered out of me, my throat dry, my heart pounding. "Please..."

"Please what?"

I didn't have an answer for that. *Please don't stop. Please don't leave. Please love me.*

There were a hundred ways to finish it, but I couldn't think beyond anything more than *please...*

Staring into vivid green eyes, I just gasped it out again. Heat built inside me, the orgasm looming in front of me, so close, so very close. I strained toward it, and as though he knew exactly what I wanted, what I needed, he let go of my right leg, smoothed a hand along my inner thigh, placed it against my belly, his thumb just brushing the curls between my thighs. "You're so close. I can feel it...your pussy is grabbing at me like a fist."

Heat rushed to my face and I groaned, looking away.

That hand that had rested on my belly slid up now, along my torso, up my neck until he caught my chin, thumb along one side, his fingers spread across my other cheek. "Look at me. I want to see what I do to you." He twisted his hips and again and I cried out, arching up as I felt a harsh, twisting spasm of pleasure ripple through me. "I want to see it in your eyes, feel it here—in your pussy."

"Drake!"

He laughed. "You make me feel, too," he said, coming back down over me, crushing me into the unyielding wood at my back. "You always did. You make me feel stupid and greedy and determined to have everything from you I can get. All your blushes, all your sighs...come for me, Shan. Let me have this."

Then he slid his hand back between us and I cried out as he started to circle the aching knot of my clitoris. Pleasure, lightning hot, ricocheted through me and I arched my neck, a soundless scream ripping out of me, like it was torn from my very soul.

Chapter Six

THE BED WAS SOFT UNDER me. At some point, he'd moved us from the living room into the bedroom and I could see the ocean, spreading out in front of me through the windows.

Drake lay behind me, his arm was hard around my waist. The heat of his body was like a furnace at my back.

For one sweet, sweet minute, I let myself just lie there and enjoy it.

In the past ten years, this was the closest to peace I'd ever come.

Actually, this was probably the most peace I'd ever known in my life period. I hadn't really been looking for peace as a kid—seashells, crabs and fun—I'd looked for those. But not peace.

What did peace matter when you're young?

Snuggling deeper into the blankets and Drake, I thought back to those days. Days I'd never thought to appreciate at the time. How can you, though?

I guess we just never think about it, never realize how wonderful it is to be able to simply spend the days on the beach, or even to go to school and have nothing more to worry about than getting good grades, talking with your friends on the bus, and whether or not you'd have enough money to buy a cute shirt with your allowance.

It had never once occurred to me how quickly it could all just...go away.

Just as it never occurred to me that I should treasure all those moments with my parents. How lucky I was that they'd been there, that they'd loved me and that they'd given up *their* dream once they realized they couldn't make it work anymore. Because they wanted to make sure I'd be able to have the things I wanted out of life.

Wiggling around, I turned to face Drake, hampered by the deadweight of his arm. Some people looked peaceful when they slept. Drake didn't. He looked like he was still working out mergers, deciphering blueprints and planning world domination via Gallagher Enterprises.

He was still damn beautiful.

Sighing, I reached up and traced my finger down the line of his nose. It wasn't a perfectly straight nose. It was just a bit crooked, right there in the middle, like it had been broken once. His lashes fluttered and a second later, his eyes opened and I found myself staring at him, his gaze hazy with sleep.

For a moment, we just looked at each other and then he blinked. "You're still here."

"Did you think I wouldn't be?"

"I thought maybe I'd dreamed it." The arm on my waist tightened and he rolled onto his back, pulling me with him.

His clothes had ended up in a trail from the living room to here sometime during the night and I'd never bothered to put anything on, either. That made this position very interesting. Bracing my hands on his chest, I sat up. I had to take a moment to appreciate the nuances of *that* particular movement, the heat centered between my thighs, the way his cock was rubbing against me, already pulsing. I felt an answering throb echo through me and my voice wasn't completely steady when I spoke. "If you were dreaming, we got a problem, because I had the same dream."

"Shared dreams. Strange stuff." His hands gripped my hips, fingers sinking in as he arched up. "Take me inside you, Shan."

My breath caught. I'd...ah. Part of me thought we'd talk some. Figure out just what was going to come next. "Now?"

"Doesn't seem like a better time." His eyes watched me, all but challenged me.

Okay. Talk could wait. A little while. We were going to have to talk, but why now?

———◆———

IT DIDN'T REALLY SEEM the time over breakfast, either, but I forced myself to do it.

With coffee in hand and scrambled eggs on a plate, I cleared my throat and made myself meet his eyes. "I don't know where any of this leaves us."

Drake had been in the middle of getting the bacon from the stove—my belly rumbled as if on cue—but at the sound of my voice, he paused. It only lasted a moment and he continued on to the table.

"Is it supposed to leave us anywhere?" he asked.

Licking my lips, I carefully said, "It feels like it should."

"Meaning...?"

"Our relationship hasn't exactly been normal." I reached for one of the pieces of bacon he'd just put on my plate, nipped off a bit at the edge. Bacon was one of the four basic food groups as far as I was concerned, but it tasted like sawdust. "I lived angry over what happened ten years ago. So angry I ended up pulling a total bitch routine just to get back to you. And..."

I stopped, blew out a sigh as I put the unfinished piece of bacon down. "I don't even know how you feel about me."

A chair scraped against the floor. There was nothing but silence for the next the thirty seconds, but I could feel the weight of his stare.

Slowly, I turned my head to look at him.

He reached for the cup of coffee and stared down into it, brooding over it like he expected to find the answers to everything inside. Caffeine did have miraculous properties, but I didn't think he'd find the answers we needed in that cup.

"I could have told you how I felt about you ten years ago," Drake said after almost a full minute passed. "I could have. But it would have been wrong."

My heart slammed against my ribs as he lifted his head. The intensity of his stare slammed into me, practically pinning me in place. "I fell in love with you that summer. And not a damn thing has changed. Not for me."

For one brief, bright moment, hope burned inside me.

Then it felt like the very world was going to crumble beneath my feet. Once again, familiar words started to echo in the back of my mind. Harsh, brittle, so very mocking. *I don't fuck naïve little virgins, Shan.*

The pain, the shame I felt then, came rushing back, every bit as deep and cutting. Slowly, I pushed back from the table. My head spun in dizzying circles and I tried to breathe in. It hurt, a band around my chest making it all but impossible to take a deep enough breath.

"Shan." His voice, low and quiet, cut through the noise in my head.

"Don't," I said, shaking my head. I turned away, desperate to be alone for a few minutes. I needed to think. I so badly needed to think. This...this should make it better, right? I'd mattered then, if he could be believed. This should make it better. So why did I feel like he just slashed my heart open all over again.

I made it two steps before he came up behind me, his arms coming around me. "Let me go," I said, forcing the words out through a throat gone tight with emotion. There was something trapped inside me. I didn't understand it. Was it a scream? Was it a sob? I didn't understand.

"No." The words were spoken against my hair. "I had to do that once—it was wrong then. Even if I hadn't been here to buy this place, I was too old for you. It was all wrong. But it didn't change how I felt. One look at you and I was done for."

"Let me go." The shaking started deep inside me and I couldn't stop it. If he didn't let me go, and *now*, I was going to break. Right here. Right now.

"Why?" He spun me around and caught my face in his hands. "You came after *me*. You came to *me* last night. You're the one who was just sitting there telling me you didn't know how I felt and now I tell you and you want me to let you go."

I blinked and when I looked back at him, it was through a veil of tears. I reached out, fumbling for anything that would push him away, anything that would give me the distance I needed to think. I just needed to think. "You're lying. You son of a bitch. You told me that night that you don't fuck naïve little virgins. Fine. I get it. I wasn't sophisticated enough, old enough for you. But don't you dare stand there and tell me you loved me when you were that cruel—"

"I don't give a damn about how *sophisticated* you were. None of that mattered to me."

His voice was like a slap in the air and I flinched.

Furious with myself, I continued to push. "So it was the age thing. How noble of you. You could flirt with me, make out with me, let me shove my hand down your pants, but the fact that I was a seventeen-year-old virgin—*that* was your stopping point. It was okay to be cruel, though."

"Oh, fuck this," he muttered.

"I don't think so." I shoved in front of him as he would have left. Pride drove me as I shoved my hands against his chest. "So it's okay to be attracted to stupid little virgin, okay to be cruel, but no fucking her, right? She's too young. Have I got it right?"

He grabbed my arms, jerked me close. "I never meant any of it to go as far as it did," he rasped, his breath coming in heavy pants against my mouth, his brow pressed to mine. "I told myself, every time, I'd end it. I'd pull back. And all I did was get tangled up in you. I didn't know how to handle..."

"What?" I demanded, my voice thick with derision. "A teenaged girl with a crush?"

"It was more than that, and you know it. It was always more with us." He crowded me back against the counter and the heat of him, the length of his body pressed to mine all but knocked the breath out of me.

"Well." I leaned back, desperate to get some room between us but all I managed to do was put myself in a position that had my pelvis pressed flush to his while I had a painfully intimate view of his face. My heart pounded, hard and fast, as I looked at him and his eyes glittered over brightly as he watched me. "I guess you'd be the better judge. I didn't have jack to compare it to, after all."

He shoved a hand into my hair, fisted it. My breath lodged in my throat as he pressed his mouth to mine. "Neither did I, darling," he rasped.

"What in the hell is that supposed to mean?"

Drake just barely lifted his head, enough that I could see his eyes, but his face filled my vision. I saw nothing but him. He had become my entire world. But then again, it felt like it had been that way from the moment I'd met him.

His hands came up and closed around my waist, boosting me up onto the counter. I felt the imprint of each finger, like it had been seared onto my skin. Felt the rub of material as he moved between my thighs. "I think you know exactly what it means."

My heart tripped inside my chest as the blood roared inside my ears.

"Spell it out." The words came from me in halting, unsteady gasps.

"You weren't the only virgin on the beach that night." His eyes cut into me. "The problem was...*you* were still a kid. I was seven years older and as much as I wanted you, I knew it wasn't right."

The mad rhythm of my heart suddenly slowed. "That..." Images flooded me. The memory of his hands on me. How it felt when he touched me. The *way* he'd touched me. "That's bullshit."

"Is it?" A mocking look entered his eyes. "You always called me the Boy Genius. You don't know how right you are, Shan. You got any idea what it's like, being eleven years old when you start high school? Graduating when you're fifteen? The girls might think you're cute...but I'm talking puppy dog cute. Girls don't want to date a kid like that. They might pat him on the head and tease him, but they don't want to *date* him."

He slid his hands down, rested them on my thighs as he studied me through veiled eyes. "I was in the same graduating class as one of my older brothers. You can imagine my...social life was more than a little awkward."

Our gazes locked, held.

Then, just like that, he turned away.

My heart stuttered, like it fumbled to even work for the next thirty seconds. Then, finally, as it settled into something close to normal rhythm, I sucked in a deep breath and forced myself to speak. "What does this have to do with anything?"

"Just how much detail do you want on this?" he asked, tipping his head back as he stared up at the exposed beams of the ceiling. "You want to hear about the gorgeous cheerleader I had a crush on my senior year? I finally hit puberty—she was dating my brother and she'd always give me a hug. You can imagine how much I liked that—right up until she told me how she thought I'd just love to date her baby sister—who was twelve."

He shot me a sardonic look. "Or maybe you'd like to hear about how my mom tried to make me go to the prom and I decided I'd get myself sick just to get out of it, so I wouldn't have to sit on the sideline, so I didn't have to have people looking at me and making fun of me—or worse, have my brother get into a fight over me...again. I calculated just exactly how much Ex-Lax I could take and make myself just this side of *too* sick. It worked so well, I did it again at my senior graduation party."

"Drake..."

He settled his hips back against the island, pinning me with a cool stare. "College was a lot of fun. All those keggers most freshman attended? The one time I tried? A girl did come on to me. She was eighteen. It was just a couple of years' difference, right? I'd actually started to look like I wasn't a kid, or so I thought. I was wrong. I woke up dressed in her cheerleader uniform and so drunk, I was sick for two days. Pictures were all over campus; for months, just seeing her was enough to make me sick."

The words were coolly delivered, his face like a stone mask. No emotion shone in his green eyes. If this had ever affected him, you couldn't tell. *I* was affected, though. The dry, almost sardonic humor in his voice cut into me and left me bleeding; but at the same time, I wanted to find that girl and bash her head against a wall.

"What was her name?" I asked.

He cocked his head and looked at me curiously. "Why?"

Baring my teeth at him, I lied. "I just wanted to know."

"It's been a while." He shrugged and looked away. "I only saw her the few times and we never had classes together."

He was lying. I saw it in his eyes. I couldn't push, either. He'd already started to regale me with more—more things I didn't want to hear. But a horrified part of me had to hear this.

How many times had I wondered what his life was like? He'd talked about his brothers, and his parents; I'd seen the affection in his eyes. He was more reluctant to talk about himself, but I'd always assumed he was just...reserved. Calm. In control.

I'd never seen the loneliness that made him into who he was.

"I graduated college without ever spending more than an hour or two alone with a girl," he said, his eyes resting on my face. I had the unsettling feeling he could see every thought I had.

I looked away, but I could still feel him watching me. Watching, waiting.

"I stayed in my room, or in the library, surrounded by my books or with my eyes glued to the computer. And every chance I had, I left campus. Most kids are desperate to get *away* once they graduate high school. All I wanted to do was go back home." He laughed softly. "Of course, that didn't happen. I graduated at nineteen and my gift was a condo in Chicago, just a few blocks from the company headquarters. I had a job waiting for me. That had always been the plan. That was just what we did. Just like my brothers, I'd work my way around the company and see where I would fit in the best."

A soft sigh slid through the room. I looked over to see him stroll over to the windows, looking cut off, completely isolated, as he stared outside. Sun shone down on the waves, glinting back faceted lights of silver and blue. "I didn't seem to fit in anywhere. Alex had gone into law and he wanted to handle our legal interests, so that's where he went. Max wanted to be more hands on, out in the field, so he does that. The hotels...that was an idea Mom and Donovan had. It was their baby, and Donovan is the one who oversees it. Gallagher Enterprises has always been about design, but they had this idea of growing, doing more. I just drifted. I never settled anywhere."

Drawn to him, I moved closer, but the look he gave me, distant and closed had me going still. "I drifted, from marketing to design, though every department we had. I went with my father to meetings, I flew out to travel with Max, I hit the hotels with Donovan. Nothing clicked. Donovan set me up on my first date, while we were in St. Augustine. He was interested in some land there, but passed it up." A sour laugh escaped him.

The sound of it cut me through. "While he was discussing business, I was out on a date. Right about the time Donovan decided this wasn't going to work out, I tried to kiss a girl for the first time. I missed her mouth altogether. The second date was one my brother Max set up and that was even worse. It got to the point to where even my mom stopped trying to set me up for dates, and my brothers outright refused to do it no matter how much she pushed them. Everybody knew it would be a disaster. I developed two obsessions—working my ass off, and locking myself in at night so I could jack off while I watched porn. It was the only way I was likely to ever get any action, so it became a fixation. Almost an addiction."

He tipped his head back and stared up at the ceiling, focusing on it. "That's how it was until around the time I turned twenty. I worked. I went home. I dropped a fortune on the best porn I could get my hands on and I pretended that was enough. I became a fucking expert at getting myself off. Then..." He blew out a breath. "Then I met Brooke."

Something hot exploded inside me. Jealousy. I recognized it for what it was, although I'd never felt it quite like this.

"I'd been working in Sales. Mom thought I'd do okay there and I did. Brooke came in and started making waves. People loved her or they hated her. I saw her and it was like my brain ceased to exist." He slid me a look.

My skin went tight as he came toward me, each step slow and steady. "I don't know if I could say I *liked* her, not looking back at it now. She treated people like shit, but she had a way of looking at people. She asked me out, not once, not twice, but three times. It took me that long to work up the courage. We went out to dinner, she talked me into going back to my place. I wasn't thinking—she finds every dirty movie I have, because I never put them up. Nobody ever came over to visit, or asked to come over, not anymore. Not even my family because I'd been shutting them out for so long."

Despite the jealousy burning in my gut over this woman I didn't know, something stirred inside me. He was staring off at nothing, his expression remote. It didn't look like this even fazed him, but I hurt for him.

"She's looking at everything and I'm ready to sink into the floor. The first woman who actually acts like I'm not an amusing little kid, not a freakish idiot—and she sees a hundred high-dollar porn movies stacked in front of a widescreen TV." He turned his head and looked at me. "Instead of walking out the door, she comes over to me and wraps her arms around my neck and laughs, tells me she'd been thinking I was all straight -aced and serious."

He was straight-laced and serious. He was also amazing, and he was mine. She'd hurt him. This woman, still faceless to me, had hurt him. I wanted to ask how, but he was still talking.

"I was so relieved about it, it takes my brain a while to catch up, then my body a while to slow down. We'd been on the couch and my hands were probably shaking—I think I'm finally going to be able to get this right, and she up and walks out the door, blows me a kiss over her shoulder. Tells me she'll see me at work. This kept up for weeks. I was too stupid to realize the games she was playing, or just how much she was messing with me. I'd gotten a promotion, moved into my own office...she comes in, tells me she wants to *congratulate* me. My mother walks in while she's under the fucking desk..." His voice trailed off and he looked at me.

I swallowed and tore my gaze away. Yeah, I could fill in those blanks on my own.

After a moment, he blew out a breath. "I thought I'd die but Mom didn't even know. When Mom left, she climbs out and hands me a movie...tells me we ought to watch it in there, have us a party."

"Was she trying to get you fired?" I demanded.

"No." He shrugged. "She was trying to fuck with the family. After we'd been...dating...or whatever we were doing about two months, my dad calls me into the office, tells me that he had done some looking into her background. Apparently her ex-husband had owned one of the smaller firms we'd bought out. He had bad ethics, cut corners we didn't like. Most of his team was great, but we wouldn't work with him so when we came on, he was pushed out. He killed himself a few weeks later and she blamed us."

Something hot and ugly twisted inside me.

"Just like I did." Turning away, I planted my hands on the counter. Over the roar of blood crashing on my ears, I couldn't even hear him say my name and I didn't hear him move. But he had.

"No. Not like you," he murmured as he closed his arms around my waist. "Never like you."

He rubbed his cheek against mine, ignoring me as I tried to pull away.

I couldn't accept the comfort he offered, but neither could I leave the warmth of his embrace. Woodenly, I stood there. "What happened?"

"I didn't believe him," Drake said, his lips brushing against my skin. "I was obsessed with her. With how I couldn't stop thinking about her, with how she made me feel. I thought I was in love with her. I told him he was full of bullshit, told him..."

I felt the muscles in his arms tighten and I stroked a hand down his arm, misery rising in me. Misery for both of us. He'd come to me, so battered inside and I hadn't realized it. Now I was the battered one. Two broken people. How could we make this work?

"I quit. Right then, right there. Told him I was going to ask her to marry me and I'd open my own place. I had money—my grandparents left each of us with chunk of change after their deaths and I *thought* I could do exactly what my dad knew how to do. But when I went to her...she laughed. She just laughed, and I didn't get it. I told her I wanted to marry her, that we belonged together. That was when she let the mask slip—she stared at me, then started to laugh. *You're an awkward boy. I had to teach you how to kiss, how to touch me. I'd probably have to teach you how to fuck and you think I'd want to stay with you?*"

He pulled away then, putting distance between us. "Don't think I don't know how much I hurt you," he said, his voice flat. "I know I did, and I *chose* to do it. I could have said I was sorry that night, the next day. I thought I was doing the right thing, keeping my distance. I didn't deserve you anyway."

I felt every inch of the distance he put between us, and the words he'd just said were like a scar on my soul. He turned and looked back at me from across the kitchen, his gaze cool and unreadable. "I never loved her. I figured that out soon enough and I got over that. It was my pride, more than anything else, and the humiliation. The words she said hurt the most, but I got over it. I put her behind me, decided I'd lose myself in business, and only business. Sex wasn't even worth the headache it had cost me. Sex wasn't worth it, trying to get involved with a woman wasn't worth it. I couldn't do it without fucking it up so why bother?"

He shrugged, a casual gesture that said much. "Dad asked me to come back, told me this..." He looked around the cottage, but I suspected he saw something more than the four walls, the golden beams overhead and the warm glow of lights. "I had to make something work. I focused on design—not the architectural part so much, but the hospitality area. I felt a tug there, thought I could make something grow there. I was going to prove myself. I was going to prove I could fit in, make it happen. Just as well as my brothers, and maybe, just as well as he did."

His tone was cool. His eyes were flat.

Yet I could practically feel the hurt inside him. This time, I didn't let the distance in his expression stop me. I went to him, sliding my arms around his waist. Pressing my face to his back, I said, "I don't think they needed you to prove anything, Drake."

"They didn't. I had to do it for me." Some of the tension drained out of him and he reached up, covered my hands with his, his thumb stroking along my skin. "That's how I ended up here. I'm the one who learned about this place. I'd been looking. It took almost two years to find the right spot. I wanted a project of my own. Something that I could do, a place I could fix up and turn around. This was going to be it, my first big project. I had it all planned out, knew how everything was going to go."

He turned and looked down at me. "Then I met you. *That* was when I figured out what love felt like. The wrong place. The wrong time. But everything about *you* felt completely right."

My heart squeezed and I couldn't take the distance between us anymore. I moved in until bare inches separated us and then I reached up, cupped his face. "If that's how you felt, then why did you push me away?"

"I just explained that." He held my wrist, his thumb sweeping along the inside. "How would you have felt if I'd slept with you that night, then you heard about the sale the next day? It was all but final, Shan. Your parents had to sell. You know that by now. The sale was pretty much a done deal. What else was I going to do?"

Staring into his eyes, I opened my mouth, words rising, trying to break free. But...I just didn't know. Groaning, I dropped my head onto his chest. There were things I wanted to say, things I wanted to do. But I didn't know where to start, or how.

His free hand slid up my back and he nuzzled the sensitive skin just below my temple. I could feel his breath stirring my hair, stirring all of me. "Are we really just going to walk away from this? From each other?" he asked softly. "What we have, what started that summer is still there. You feel it. I feel it."

I lifted my face to his.

Reaching up, I touched my fingers to his lips. "I don't think I can walk away."

"Then we need to figure out where all of this leaves us."

With a knot in my throat, I nodded.

Some of those words I had trapped inside finally broke free. I *knew* what I wanted. *Who* I wanted. I could tell him. Give him that, at least.

Except, when I braced myself, opened my mouth to speak, the phone rang, the sounds of something rich and melodic drifting through the air. Old style jazz. My father had loved it.

"Mom...oh. Dad. Hey...what...?"

His hands fell away from me, a hard, heavy tension slamming into him. I backed away, dread curdling inside me as he paced along the floor, listening. He made a few soft murmurs, stopped once and lifted his face to the sky. Then, stopping near a glass-fronted cabinet, he stopped.

I jumped as he slammed a fist into the glass, shards breaking, the cracks splintering up through it. "No. It's nothing. I'm fine. How bad?"

There was an odd, strained silence, and then he nodded. "I...yes. I'll be there."

He turned to look at me but my gaze was locked on his hand, the rivulets of blood dripping down. It held me mesmerized. Frozen.

Blood. Slick and red.

My belly started to churn.

I'd seen a fist, streaked red with blood, driving into my father's face. My mother's belly. Mine.

The blood, the sight of it, tried to push me back into a place I couldn't go and this time, I fought against it. As black dots edged in around my vision, I forced it back. I moved into the kitchen and pulled some paper towels off the roll. Thinly, I said, "You're bleeding."

Drake looked down at his hand, his gaze puzzled like he hadn't even noticed.

Maybe he hadn't.

I moved back over to him and caught his hand, pressing the paper towel to it and stopping the flow of blood. Over it, he looked at me. "I have to go to Chicago. My mom is in the hospital."

"Is..." Unable to stop myself, I looked back at his bloody hand, felt time spinning away again. Voices rose in the back of my head while blood splattered across the veil of my memories.

Hands tangling in my hair. A voice in my ear—*scream, little girl*. The tire iron raised.

My lungs burned, aching for another breath. I pushed the memories out at the same time I expelled the air trapped in my lungs.

Instead of letting myself see the red, see the *blood*, I looked at his sweater instead, at his wrists, at his chest, at my own hand. "Is she okay?"

"I don't know." He looked for me, caught my chin. His hand was icy against my skin.

"Come with me. Please."

Scream, little girl—

I wanted to. It was trapped inside me.

But I didn't. Go with Drake. To Chicago. I wanted to say yes. I could handle going to Chicago, even if I had to walk through the doors of a hospital, relive the nightmare that crowded my head every time those familiar scents assaulted me. I could do it. I wanted to, wanted to be there for him.

One thing, so small as to be insignificant, stopped me. It was just a piece of paper. I could tear it up and forget I'd seen it. The mail lost it, the cat ate it—no, I didn't have a cat, but nobody needed to know.

But those details had the name, the date, the time. I'd face him again, the man who'd fisted his hand in my hair and told me to scream, just so he could beat my father, my mother. Face the man who'd dragged me off the street and forced me into a dirty, stinking trunk. I'd been trapped in there for hours while he drove around, convinced I was going to die. I had to face the man who'd told his partner to do it, to kill my parents.

I opened my mouth, tried to force the words out. They caught in my throat and I just couldn't *speak*.

I can't. That was all I had to say.

Five days.

I only had five days.

Swallowing, I asked, "How long will it take?"

"It could take a few days."

Turning away, I gripped the counter. "I can't come until Monday evening."

A humorless laugh filled the air. "Wow. Thanks."

"Drake, I..."

"No. It's okay." Just like that, he turned his back on me. The action cut me to the very bottom of my soul. "Well...fuck. Here I go thinking we're trying to make this work. But yeah. Monday."

"Drake, *wait*," I said, shoving myself toward him on stiff, awkward legs.

"No. My mom, my family needs me."

My mom needs *me.* And beyond that, I had to do this...for *me.* Every time I faced him, I tried to pretend I'd get stronger, be less afraid. It never happened, I was always afraid. But I had to try.

Tell him. The words were there. They were *there.* But I couldn't force them out. I was frozen. All I could say was, "Drake, please."

By time I managed to unfreeze myself, even a little, he was already gone, striding out of the cottage like demons were at his heels. He didn't slow down and I heard an engine roar before I even hit the front door.

Chapter Seven

MY CALLS WENT TO VOICE mail.

Part of me wanted to be pissed. But then again, I'd walked away in Philadelphia.

I tried texting him, half expecting him to ignore me. I didn't go into detail, just kept it simple. *I'd go right now, if I could. I have something I have to take care of first.*

He did respond, to my surprise.

You don't owe me explanations. I hope you understand, but I need to focus on my family right now. If you want to join me in Chicago, just let my assistant at the Cove know. She's aware that you're a friend of mine and I'll leave instructions with her on where you can find me. She'll get you a ticket once she hears from you.

I made a face. I could get my own damn ticket.

For now, I had to get out of here, though. The silence of the place closed around me and threatened to drive me mad.

It seemed the two of us might forever be dancing around the edge, never able to fully give the other what we both needed.

I needed to get in touch with Mom, make sure everything was set up for the trip to Florida. Staring at the phone, I thought of things I wanted to tell him, explanations I could offer. If he'd called, if he'd answered, I would have tried. But a text message wasn't exactly the right venue for saying...*I have to go to Florida and make sure one of my attackers stays in jail, make sure he pays for what he did to my family.*

Besides, Drake really didn't need that weight on his brain, did he?

Instead, I simply texted him a simple message: *I'll miss you.*

It was nothing but the truth. I'd missed him every day for the past ten years. It didn't matter that it would only be a few days before I'd see him. I was still going to miss him. At least I'd have something to look forward to, other than dread, as I thought about the upcoming week.

I watched my screen, waiting for a response.

There wasn't one, though.

It left a void in me. An awful, gaping void.

———◉———

MY MOTHER PICKED ME up from the airport the next day, just before noon. My head still felt like it was stuffed with cotton, but less achy. My eyes protested the sunlight. My body protested movement and even touch, but as Mom wrapped her arms around me, I sighed and tucked my head against her shoulder. For a minute, I could pretend I was a kid again, and she was one of the few people in the world who could make everything better.

"You look like you haven't slept well in a week," she murmured.

Then I'd done wonders with my make-up because it had been a lot longer than a week. With an easy smile, I pulled back and shrugged. "It's that time of year. Almost through it, right?"

She sighed and brushed my hair back. "Shannon, baby, sooner or later, you have to move past this. I..." She closed her eyes, took a deep breath. "In my gut, I think we have to face the truth. I don't see them making Young serve his entire sentence."

Bitter words brewed inside me. I kept them locked where they were. "I know." Weariness dogged me as I edged around, pulling my wheeled suitcase behind me. "I'm surprised they didn't let him go last year. That doesn't mean I'm not going to try."

"Of course not." She helped me maneuver the suitcase in. Normally, I would have argued with her, but I still felt like hell and I didn't want her to ask, didn't want to go into detail about the fall, or anything. Especially Drake. "You wouldn't know how to give up. You got that from me."

I should have realized then, that she was going to meddle.

But she waited, until we were pulling away from the airport, until we were far away from the rush of the city and lost in the winding streets that led to the place she'd called home for the past few years. Forty minutes of peace, forty minutes of silence lulled me.

Then, her voice level and soft, she asked, "So...who is Mike?"

My hands, clasped in my lap, tightened until I'd made the knuckles go white. "Ah...just a friend."

"Hmmm. My daughter who hasn't had a guy friend that I'm aware of since...well...*ever*...has a guy friend she trusts well enough to help her out after a head injury, one she didn't tell *me* about, might I add? And I'm supposed to believe he's just a friend?" A serene smile curved her lips as she shook her head. "I'm not buying it. How long have you known him? Where did you meet?"

My mouth went dry. Panic crashed into me. How did I answer that? How would she feel? She'd never seemed to carry the rage inside her like I had, but how did I know this wouldn't hurt her?

"Work," I said, forcing the word out. "We met through my last job. I've known him a while."

Her brow furrowed. "But I thought you weren't there long. Didn't you tell me you quit? Although, honestly Shan, I know you *want* to work, but you can't settle. It seems like you have an awful time figuring out what you *want*."

I didn't respond.

"Honey?"

"Yes?" I squeezed my eyes closed, face averted so she couldn't read anything there.

"Do you know what you want?"

An image of Drake, of that lovely, sprawling little place he'd created on the beach flashed through my mind. Both of the dreams I'd thought I'd lost. But if I could only have one?

I'd take Drake.

"I know what I want, Mom. It's just...sometimes knowing isn't enough."

She reached over and covered my fisted hands with one of hers, gave them a quick squeeze. "You have so much of your dad in you. Such a dreamer. But you're smart, so much more determined. You can make your dreams come true if you want it enough, if you're willing to fight hard enough."

She let go and put her hand back on the wheel, her gaze still on the road. "So, you going to give me any more information on this...Mike? His voice was awfully familiar."

I bit back a groan. "It's still kind of up in the air."

"So basically, you're not ready to tell me." She wrinkled her nose. "You never did like to talk about any guy you were interested in. Not that there have been many. The only one that ever caught your eye for longer than a minute was Drake Gallagher."

Before I could stop it, my head spun around and I gaped at her.

She laughed softly. "Oh, come on. Are you really surprised that I saw it? I knew, from the get-go. I wanted to warn you, but I didn't want you angry at me and your father...or even with Drake himself. I think it made him nervous. He was such a shy thing—you remember Stella, the girl we'd bring in to help with meetings? How she flirted with any man in pants? She'd teased him something terrible and he'd go almost as red as his hair and he acted so stiff and proper around her. Last I heard, she still works there, at the new place. He offered to keep on the old staff if they wanted. She's worked her way up, helps manage the place now. Settled down, too. Got married, has a child or two."

All of that flew through my head, without connecting.

"You knew about Drake," I said, my lips numb.

"That you had a crazy crush on him? Yes." She shot me an odd look before focusing back on the road. "Why is that such a surprise?"

Shaking my head, I looked back out the window as fields flew by. What would she do, I wondered, if I told her that it was more than a *crush* I had on Drake—that even now the very mention of his name made my heart race, my knees melt and my brain just turn off.

I didn't know.

And now wasn't the time to think about it either.

I had to get through the next few days first. Then I'd go be with Drake. Then, if I could find the brain cells, I'd figure out how to handle telling my mom.

———◉———

LIFE IN JAIL HADN'T treated Todd Young kindly.

This was the first year I'd actually been able to see him clearly, though. To see him and realize there was something behind the monster from my dreams.

Ten years ago, when he'd been arrested, his lawyers had put him in a nice suit, cut his dark hair, so he made the impression of a nice, trustworthy, all-around good boy. He'd made a mistake, sure, but didn't everybody?

The judge hadn't bought it.

He gave a speech more by rote than anything else. He'd been long, lean and lanky before. Now he was solid, through and through, with heavy muscle. His cheekbones pressed against his skin like razors and I could see the prison tattoos peeking out from under his shirt, along his neck. His hair was greasy and thin, lines fanning out from his eyes.

None of that meant much.

His eyes were dead. *That* was the disturbing thing. Those eyes were like dead bits of glass in his face, uncaring and sharp. Looking at those mean eyes was enough to make my skin crawl, but I didn't flinch.

I'd known so much fear because of this man.

I'd hated, so much, because of this man.

And there he sat, staring at me like I was nothing. He'd tried to *make* me into nothing. Worse...for so many years, I'd let him. I'd slid into the shadows and barely even made a pretense at life.

The hot, potent anger that I'd thought had died flooded me. It was the anger I'd felt when I thought of Drake, the anger that I'd thought had died. Anger that had been directed at the wrong people for far too long.

Now, as I stared at the man who'd helped destroy my life, I let the anger burn the fear until it was cowering inside me. I looked at him and I didn't flinch. Not once as he stared at me. I didn't look away as they called my name and not as I spoke about what had been done. To me, to my family, to my father. I told how he'd whispered in my ear, how he'd laughed the few times he'd made me scream.

"It's still vivid, even now," I said, looking from the people in their nice suits with their unaffected smiles back to Young. None of them would be touched by this, save for him, my mom and me. We were the ones who would feel this.

Just as we were the ones who still felt the ripples from that day long ago.

Ripples that even now were interfering with my life.

Abruptly, I started to laugh.

"Is something funny?"

I looked up at the man in front of me.

"No," I said quietly. "This is all crazy and insane and tragic. I'm *here*...again, letting that monster dictate how I live my life. What I do with my life. Who I'll be with."

I was here, in a room with a man I hated, instead of being in Chicago with the man I loved, the man who needed me. "There's a man in Chicago right now who needs me with him," I said softly. "He wanted me with him. I had to put my life on hold."

I looked away, stared at my mom for a minute and then looked at the bland beige walls, the bland, insipid pictures. "My life was spun around into hell the moment that monster over there grabbed me and threw me into a trunk. I remember every time he hit me—sixteen times," I murmured. A phantom ache rose from my belly. "They hit my parents even more than that and they left bruises and broken bones. You'd think that getting *out* alive would be enough. That sooner or later, you can shut out the sound of *hearing* those bones break. That you might forget the sound of his voice in your ear as he told you to scream, just so he'd have a reason to hit your parents, beat them in front you."

I shook my head, looking at Young. "You don't forget. He's spent all these years in prison. Whether he serves any more time or not, it's not enough."

Silence fell, heavy and thick. I felt the weight of their gazes on me but I didn't look away from Young. He was staring at the table now. "Can't you look at me now?" I asked, an edge cutting into my voice. "Can't you look at the *little girl* you grabbed from the street and threw into a trunk? My life—the life I knew—ended that day. You shattered it. I wake up from nightmares, find myself on the floor, tucked against a wall because I'm afraid you'll find me, you son of a bitch."

He jerked, then, like somebody had hit him.

It was the first time I'd ever spoken to him.

"You can't even look at me now. Coward."

Feeling like I might puke, like my head might explode, I looked away. My hands shook, my belly pitched and rolled. Staring at the men and women who'd decide if he'd *paid his debt* to society, I shook my head. "You get to decide now, if he's done enough. If he's paid his debt, if he's been reformed and if he's *sorry* for what he did." A bitter laughed escape me. "He's not sorry. That coward can't even look me in the face, can't acknowledge what he did. You let him go now, he'll just do it to another child, destroy another family. Sleep well, with that thought in your head. But I'm not going to let him control my life. Not anymore."

Chapter Eight

A HOT BATH, A GLASS of wine, and I slept like the dead. My mother had been oddly silent on the drive from the prison back into town, her expression pensive, her face unreadable. We'd had dinner and then we'd both gone to our separate rooms at the hotel. We were both too worn out for anything more than that.

A bleary look at the clock on the table told me that had been some eight hours ago. It was early, too early. Four forty-two in the morning.

So why, pray-tell was there somebody knocking on my door?

I ignored the first knock and flipped onto my belly, shoving my face into a pillow.

The doombringer didn't go away. The second knock was louder and I groaned, lifted my head up and glared toward the dark maw where I thought the door was.

If I got up, I just might hurt whoever was at the door.

It was just how it was.

A third knock decided the person's fate.

Stumbling out of bed, I knuckled at my eyes and managed to get the door open. Just as Drake lifted his fist to knock again.

I gaped at him.

His hands came up and caught my face. Any questions I might have had died as he kissed me.

When I went to pull back, he just pulled me against him and moved us inside, kicking the door shut. Velvety darkness wrapped around us. With my mind still hazed from sleep, it was easy to think this was all a dream.

That is, until he hit the lights and lifted his head to stare at me, his eyes stark, almost haunted.

"Why the hell didn't you tell me?"

I blinked, confused. I either needed more sleep or caffeine.

Pushing against his chest, I wiggled away from him and made my way over to the kitchenette and studied the Keurig. It was just as easy as the one I had at home, but just then, it struck me as very confusing. Water. Coffee. Cup. Button. Okay, I remembered now.

"Tell you what?" I asked once I pushed the start button. *Hurry*, I thought silently. I needed caffeine, so bad. Flicking him a look, I frowned. "Why are you here? Isn't your mom in the hospital?"

"Yes. Her surgery is tomorrow. I fly back this afternoon. Now answer me." He closed the distance between us with two long strides. "Why didn't you tell me?"

I rubbed my eyes. "Tell you what? How did you know where I was?"

"Tell me about the parole meeting," he practically snarled. His hand shot out, planted against the wall by my head. My heart jumped into my throat as I looked up, met his eyes. "As to how...your *mom* told me. I called, while you were in the middle of testifying. She went to silence the phone and accidentally hit talk. I practically had a front row seat for half of it."

My stomach dropped out.

"Oh." Turning my head, I stared at the little black coffee maker, the wisps of steam rising as the coffee began to stream out. But I didn't need the caffeine any more. My mind was achingly, painfully clear. Swallowing around the knot, I continued to stare at the cup—the Harry Potter travel mug my mother had picked up for me when she went to Universal Studios a few months ago on a wild lark with Paul. That was what she'd called it. A wild lark. "When did she talk to you?"

"What does it matter?" he demanded. "I want to know why *you* weren't the one telling me."

Sighing, I shifted my gaze back around to him, met those haunted green eyes. Haunted, dark. I lifted a hand and touched his cheek, half-afraid to do that. He caught my palm in his hand, pressed it closer. That alone eased the ragged ache inside. "And when was I supposed to tell you, Drake? You were rushing out the door, worried about your mom. You were angry with me—"

"I didn't kn—"

Pressing my fingers to his mouth, I silenced the words I didn't need to hear. "I know that. I know, and I understand. But what did you expect me to do—blurt out that I couldn't be with you when your mom was sick because I had to go to Florida and make sure one of the men responsible for killing my dad stayed in jail? When was the ideal time?"

Drake closed his eyes, pressed his forehead to mine. "Damn it, Shan."

"If I was going to tell you, it should have been *before* but oddly, it never came up." I forced myself to smile. "There was that weird thing with me getting a concussion, you not knowing anything about what had happened, then us crawling all over each other."

"You could have called me."

"No." I rubbed my lips against his, felt them part. "That isn't really something you say over the phone, in an email. Besides..."

I pulled back, tucked my head against his shoulder. "It doesn't matter if it's been ten minutes since it all happened, or ten years. I'm still raw. I can't think about it without freezing—it takes me a while just to get past that, takes my throat a while to unlock. I need to give my heart time to slow and wait for my hands to stop sweating. The first few years, I had to have meds for anxiety and I had panic attacks just thinking about looking at one of them. It's better now, but it's a knee-jerk thing that hits me at weird times. I need a few seconds to breathe through it before I can talk about it."

"And I walked out before you had a chance to breathe," he whispered against my temple.

"You're here now. I've had a chance to breathe."

He tugged me closer. "I'm an ass."

I started to say something, then I shrugged.

"Maybe. But you were worried about your mom." I stroked a hand up his chest, fisted it over his heart. "I figure maybe we're even now. Well, maybe not even. I had a ten-year hate-on for you, but maybe this evens the scales a little."

He boosted me up onto the counter. "There aren't any scales. I was a bastard then and wasn't honest. We started over." His eyes narrowed on mine. "Aren't you going to yell at me, throw something?"

"I think I'm yelled out for now." Smoothing my hands down his shirt, I shrugged and smiled up at him. "We can pretend to fight, though. Then have crazy hot make-up sex."

A sleepy-lidded look came across his face and he pushed his hands under my sleepshirt, found me naked. "Crazy hot make-up sex without the fight? Fine. I'm mad at you and you're mad at me...now we have crazy hot make-up sex?"

My breath hitched. I caught the hem of his t-shirt, dragged it up but he didn't let me pull it off. He was too busy fighting with his belt buckle, then his zipper. A minute later, his cock was freed and I went to reach for him as heat flared to life inside me. His hand closed around my wrist, pinning it to down to my side before I could touch him. He pulled my hips to the very edge of the counter with his other hand and I felt the head of him there, right against me.

"We start over," he muttered, leaning into me.

"Over." My heart stuttered as I watched him sink inside, my flesh stretching tight to welcome him. Pleasure ripped at me as he sank deep and hard, need was a scream when he withdrew. *More...more...more...*

A sob of despair rose in me and I wiggled, trying to get closer. Staring down at him, desperate, I whispered, "Please."

His cock was thick, wet from me and I gasped in relief as he surged back inside.

Over and over.

It felt...new. Not like the first time. Better. No secrets, no shadows. Emotion welled in me and I lifted my face to his, needing more.

He gave it, his lips crushing to mine. His tongue came into my mouth, echoing the rhythm of his cock, a double pleasure.

His hand fell away from my wrist, moving to cup my ass. Braced by the strength of his hands, I lay there, helpless, full with him and delight, as he drove himself inside me.

It was beautiful.

It was blissful.

And it ended all too soon. The hunger was too much for both of us and I felt the urgency in him, felt the echo of it within me. "Shan...fuck. I need you," he rasped, tearing his mouth from mine to mutter in my ear. "I love you. I love you..."

The words exploded inside me and I cried out, all but dying in his arms.

Clutching him to me, I whispered those very words, the words I kept inside me all this time, to his mouth. "I love you."

We were lost then, lost in each other and for the first time in too many years, the past and its shadows fell away from me.

We were all that mattered. The two of us, and that very moment.

———————⬤———————

I STOOD IN FRONT OF the hospital with him that day. It was later. We hadn't had much sleep. I needed more coffee and I was terrified to take the next step.

But it was time.

His hand closed warmly over mine.

"You don't have to come inside," he said softly. "I have to be there. The cardiac surgeon is going over things and I need to know what to expect, how she's going to do. But, you can go to the hotel."

The doors were like eyes, staring into my soul, exposing all those weaknesses, all those fears.

But this was just a building. It was a place where sick people went, a place where injured people were brought. I'd lain in a hospital when they told me about my father and that had given birth to that fear. I couldn't conquer it by staying at a hotel. And I couldn't help Drake—I couldn't *be* with Drake—if I walked away. If I was going to fix myself, it had to start somewhere. It had to start here.

"I'm coming in." I looked up at him. "Just make sure you stay close."

"For the rest of your life, if I have anything to say about it."

Join The Newsletter[1]

---

1. http://www.shilohwalker.com/website/
newsletter-author-shiloh-walker/

Vicious Vixen

© 2008 Shiloh Walker

He's given one chance at redemption—hers and his.

HIRED KILLER, VIXEN Markham doesn't have any illusions about life or love. Unable to trust even the one man she lets into her heart, she makes a decision that she'll regret for the rest of her life—which won't be much longer by the looks of things. Loaded with vengeance and a small arsenal of weapons, she's ready to face up to her past and say goodbye to her future, until she's confronted by a pair of eyes she could never forget.

Graeme Mackenzie Lawson lived a hard life. Hard on himself and harder on those who got in his way. Betrayed and murdered, he's given one chance at redemption—but not for himself—for the woman he loved, the woman who killed him.

Can he keep Vixen safe, when she seems determined to lose her life—and her soul?

Enjoy the following excerpt for Vicious Vixen:

SHE'D BEEN IN THE SMALL, mid-scale apartment for just over a week. On one side lived a detective. On the other side lived a nurse. She hadn't seen much of them and preferred to keep it that way. She kept a low profile, low enough that there hadn't ever been mention of her in any of the investigations surrounding Hawthorne.

Which was a damn good thing with a detective living on one side of her. A lot of people in her position wouldn't want to sleep with a cop just on the other side of the wall. But Vixen didn't have any reason to worry being this close to a cop. She actually preferred having one close by her safe place—just another safeguard against Hawthorne prying into her life. He was far less likely to have his men go in and set up bugs when there was a chance a cop would notice.

So she didn't mind the cop. Vixen was glad she rarely saw her neighbors. She wasn't the friendly type, and liked it that way.

The apartment across from her had been vacant for a few weeks, but judging by the sounds coming from behind the door, that had changed. She pushed her key into the deadbolt and turned it, but just before she could slip inside and shut herself off, the door behind her opened.

She didn't even have to see him.

Her body knew.

Her heartbeat sped up, her hands went damp and her knees got weak.

Shit, she thought silently.

"Hello again."

His voice was just as perfect now as it had been when he crashed into her less than an hour earlier. Slowly, she turned her head and met his gaze over her shoulder. "You."

He smiled. "Do you believe in coincidences?"

"No." She unlocked the second lock and opened the door. As she slipped inside, she glanced back at him.

"Are you always this friendly?" he asked, still giving her that inviting, open grin.

"Yes. Are you?"

He laughed. The sound of it was like velvet rubbing over her skin and she suppressed a shiver. "Actually, no."

Go inside, her head said firmly. Shut the door. Get your head on straight. But instead, she lingered in the doorway and studied his face. It was a nice face, she decided. The whole package was nice—broad shoulders, narrow waist, lean hips. Oh yes, very nice. With a body like that, he could be outright ugly from the shoulders up and he'd still have women checking him out.

But the face was every bit as nice as the body. Narrow, with elegant, clean lines, a wide mouth that she imagined knew how to kiss very well. Earlier, he'd worn a pair of mirrored shades that had kept her from seeing his eyes and he hadn't gotten around to taking them off yet.

"Why am I getting the special treatment?"

One of those wide shoulders moved in a negligent shrug. He reached up to push his sunglasses onto his head as he replied, but whatever he said fell on completely deaf ears. Vixen's heartbeat faltered. Her hands were all slippery with sweat and blood roared in her ears.

His eyes.

Everything else faded away as she stared into eyes the color of blue neon. Eyes that color couldn't possibly be real, although she'd once known a man who had eyes that same impossible shade. She stumbled backward, fumbled the door open and all but fell inside. Shoving it closed behind her, she fumbled with the locks, a sob catching in her throat. Finally, she managed to secure them but her fingers shook too much to put the chain on. Blinded by tears, she pressed her forehead against the door and tried to breathe.

Tried to breathe, but couldn't.

His eyes.

Damn it, looking into his eyes, for just a second, it had been like she was looking into Graeme's eyes once more. Guilt churned in her gut, but the guilt wasn't what had her shaking like a leaf. It was grief.

She half-fell, half-leaned against the wall, slowly sliding down until she was crouched in the corner. Drawing her knees up to her chest, she hid her face against her legs and tried to block off the torrent of memories storming through her...

Her soul mate...or her downfall?

Look for Shiloh's Latest...
<u>Spectre</u>[1]

Spectre

I WASN'T EVEN A MAN when I took a life for the first time, although you couldn't say I was a child. If I'd ever had a childhood, it hadn't lasted long. My father, may he rot in hell, had seen to that. I took his life as well and that, too, happened before I was old enough to be considered a grown man. I never regretted it for a second.

That path almost led to my own grave, and would have, if I hadn't stumbled across somebody who was as different from my father as day was from night. Sarge had seen the monster lurking inside, so he took control, gave me guidelines, rules, so I wouldn't be the monster my father had planned.

It worked. I restrained the worst of my rage and honed the skills that had been drilled into me—theft, stealth... assassination. The broken child ceased to exist and I became Spectre, an assassin spoken of in whispers, hired to take out the worst of humanity.

Then I was sent to kill her...and my world came to a screeching halt.

Tia

It's taken a long time, but I finally had a nice, steady routine. I stopped trying to conform to the neurotypicals of the world and found my own normal.

Normal went out the window when I walked into my kitchen and found a strange (hot), dangerous looking (so fricking hot) man drugging my new dog.

It probably wasn't the smartest thing to leap at him like a banshee and attack, but that's what I did.

When my attempt to wreck the vehicle was averted, my kidnapper didn't hurt or threaten me. In fact, he told me he wanted to protect me.

This (hot) guy had to be crazy. But if he was crazy, what did that make me? Because I believed him. More, I found myself seeing something beyond the rigid, blank mask he wore.

THE VIRGIN

He kept trying to push me away, but I couldn't seem to keep my distance. He calls himself a monster...but when I look at him, that isn't what I see. I just see him...and I know he's meant to be mine.

Warning: This isn't a snuggly, comfy read. The male MC is a hired killer, while the heroine is neuro-atypical. Some dark material is involved—the hero kidnaps the heroine. There's also violence when he goes on a rampage against those who put a contract on her. Also references of abuse (not against the heroine). Also very graphic, erotic scenes with minor bondage play.

Read More[2]

2. https://www.shilohwalker.com/website/books/spectre/

About

SHILOH WALKER HAS BEEN writing since she was a kid. She fell in love with vampires with the book Bunnicula and has worked her way up to the more...ah...serious works of fiction. Once upon a time she worked as a nurse, but now she writes full time and lives with her family in the Midwest. She writes romantic suspense and contemporary romance, and urban fantasy under her penname, J.C. Daniels[1]. Follow her on Twitter[2], BookBub[3] & Facebook[4]. Read more about her work at her website[5]. Sign up for her newsletter[6] and have a chance to win a monthly giveaway.

---

1. http://jcdanielsblog.com/

2. https://twitter.com/walkershiloh

3. https://www.bookbub.com/authors/shiloh-walker

4. http://www.facebook.com/AuthorShilohWalker?ref=tn_tnmn

5. http://shilohwalker.com/

6. http://www.shilohwalker.com/website/newsletter-author-shiloh-walker/

Look for other titles by Shiloh

The McKays

Headed For Trouble[7]

The Trouble With Temptation[8]

The Barnes Brothers

Wrecked[9]

Razed[10]

Busted[11]

Ruined[12]

Contemporary Standalone Titles

Beg Me[13]

Tempt Me[14]

Beautiful Scars[15]

A Forever Kind of Love[16]

Playing for Keeps[17]

No Longer Mine[18]

You Own Me[19]

Her Best Friend's Lover[20]

7. http://www.shilohwalker.com/website/new-releases/headed-for-trouble-southern-romance/

8. http://www.shilohwalker.com/website/meet-the-mckays/the-trouble-with-temptation/

9. http://www.shilohwalker.com/website/wrecked/

10. http://www.shilohwalker.com/website/whats-new/razed/

11. http://www.shilohwalker.com/website/whats-new/busted/

12. http://www.shilohwalker.com/website/new-releases/ruined/

13. http://www.shilohwalker.com/website/?page_id=12724

14. http://www.shilohwalker.com/website/bookshelf/boundtemptations/

15. http://www.shilohwalker.com/website/2012/04/beautiful-scars/

16. http://www.shilohwalker.com/website/?page_id=18525

17. http://www.shilohwalker.com/website/?page_id=401

18. http://www.shilohwalker.com/website/?page_id=433

19. http://www.shilohwalker.com/website/bookshelf/you-own-me/

20. http://www.shilohwalker.com/website/bookshelf/her-best-friends-lover/

THE VIRGIN

The Ash Trilogy
If You Hear Her[21]
If You See Her[22]
If You Know Her[23]
The Secrets & Shadows Series
Burn For Me[24]
Break For Me[25]
Long For Me[26]
Deeper Than Need[27]
Sweeter Than Sin[28]
Darker Than Desire[29]
The FBI Psychics
The Missing[30]
The Departed[31]
The Reunited[32]
The Protected[33]
The Unwanted[34]
The Innocent[35]

---

21. http://www.shilohwalker.com/website/books-by-series/the-ash-trilogy/

22. http://www.shilohwalker.com/website/books-by-series/the-ash-trilogy/

23. http://www.shilohwalker.com/website/books-by-series/the-ash-trilogy/

24. http://www.shilohwalker.com/website/secrets-and-shadows/

25. http://www.shilohwalker.com/website/secrets-and-shadows/

26. http://www.shilohwalker.com/website/secrets-and-shadows/

27. http://www.shilohwalker.com/website/secrets-and-shadows/

28. http://www.shilohwalker.com/website/secrets-and-shadows/

29. http://www.shilohwalker.com/website/secrets-and-shadows/

30. http://www.shilohwalker.com/website/books-by-series/the-fbi-psychics/

31. http://www.shilohwalker.com/website/books-by-series/the-fbi-psychics/

32. http://www.shilohwalker.com/website/books-by-series/the-fbi-psychics/

33. http://www.shilohwalker.com/website/books-by-series/the-fbi-psychics/

34. http://www.shilohwalker.com/website/books-by-series/the-fbi-psychics/

SHILOH WALKER

And more[36]

35. http://www.shilohwalker.com/website/books-by-series/the-fbi-psychics/

36. *http://www.shilohwalker.com/website/bookshelf/*

CPSIA information can be obtained
at www.ICGtesting.com
Printed in the USA
LVHW021109060721
691954LV00003B/388